HAMLET HAD AN UNCLE
A Comedy of Honor

by Branch Cabell

HAMLET HAD AN UNCLE

THE KING WAS IN HIS COUNTING HOUSE

THE NIGHTMARE HAS TRIPLETS:

    SMIRT

    SMITH

    SMIRE

THESE RESTLESS HEADS

SPECIAL DELIVERY

LADIES AND GENTLEMEN

by James Branch Cabell

BIOGRAPHY OF THE LIFE OF MANUEL

PREFACE TO THE PAST

HAMLET HAD AN UNCLE

UNCLE

A Comedy of Honor

by

BRANCH CABELL

"Even with the very comment of thy soul
Observe my uncle."

DECORATED BY CHARLES CHILD

FARRAR & RINEHART, INC.

NEW YORK   TORONTO

For

THE FORGOTTEN MAN

Here is your story steadfastly retold
And freed of fancy, seeking nor to lend
Music where music was not, nor to mold
Less frankly your remissions, but to mend,
Even as you mended, error, and to hold
Truth as you held it even to the end.

"The slaying of an enemy, even if he were taken at a disadvantage, was not thought wrong by the Norse, provided that no attempt were made to keep the killing a secret; but it brought about a 'blood-feud,' which the dead man's nearest of kin were bound in honour to follow up. This could be honourably settled in two ways: 1. By the slayer himself being slain. 2. By the payment of 'blood-money,' or 'weregild,' or 'compensation,' or 'boot,' as it was variously called, to the nearest of adult male kin. Either course was permissible; but for a man not to take any action when his kinsman was slain was considered disgraceful."—GEORGE AINSLIE HIGHT.

"Divorce was easy to get among the Vikings, for 'if a man desires to separate from his wife, he shall declare himself separated so that each of them may hear the other's voice, and have witnesses present' (Gulathing Law, 54; Frostalthing Law, 11, 14); nor did this 'separating' prevent either party from marrying afterwards."—SIR G. W. DASENT.

"Perhaps the most beautiful, touching, and unselfish trait in the character of man of which we have any record is the ancient custom of foster-brotherhood, which prevailed among the earlier Norse tribes, when valiant men made an agreement, after passing under three *jardarmen* (or 'necklaces of earth'), that the comrade who lived the longest should avenge the other with weapons, not sparing even his own relatives."—PAUL B. DU CHAILLU.

PREFACE

"Thus the native hue of resolution
Is sicklied o'er with the pale cast of thought."

PREFACE

The story of Hamlet, in a perverted form, is not unfamiliar to the more highly cultured of our literati, even in America. As has been said in another place, his fame is world-wide—and completely mendacious.

Entire libraries, one repeats here, have been written about the Hamlet whom Shakespeare, to every intent, invented; the Hamlet whom ten generations have invested with an infinity of traits, doubts, philosophies and actions of which Hamlet never heard; the Hamlet who has moved his unarithmeticable billions of theatre-goers: but not any book by an American, so far as extends my knowledge, has been given up to the Hamlet who once figured in history.

The phrase "figured in history" has been selected, by prolonged thoughtfulness, from out of a jostle of candidates, forasmuch as the otherwise unemployed have shown us, plausibly, that Hamlet never lived,—somewhat as, with an equal speciousness, it has been proved that neither Jesus nor Napoleon existed. At all events, each one of the trio once occupied his conceded niche in that most imposing edifice which mankind in general had agreed to accept as a temple devoted to history, but have since re-dedicated (with unhumanistic loud revels) to a barbarian deity termed de-bunking; and out of which Hamlet, after a tenancy of some nine hundred years, was evicted, neither by irreligion nor quibbles, nor by the glib zeal of the fearlessly half-educated. Hamlet was put out of history by the genius of Shakespeare.

So far as goes human evidence, a flesh-and-blood Hamlet did prosper, in point of fact, among the Vikings, during the unhappy heyday of Justinian the Second down in Byzantium; and he got the throne of Jutland but a few years before the Saracen armies of Musa had quite finished their overrunning of Spain. So far as goes the result, this Hamlet has been made famous all over the world in the same while that, through a toplofty paradox, he has been forgotten almost completely; for a superb lie arose —somehow—behind multitudinous footlights; and before its splendor the truth skulked away into footnotes.

For the problem, whence and through what transitions came into being the plot of "The Tragedy of Hamlet, Prince of Denmark"? caution can but refer curiosity to the wild guessing of sedate specialists in such dry-as-dust matters. The plot (as these authorities inform us, a bit variously) may have been concocted by Shakespeare, in some one of his less logical moments; or by Thomas Kyd; or by that yet more widely gifted writer, Anon. The point, for our present purpose, is merely that whoever put together the superb crazy-quilt made it up, virtually, out of the whole cloth.

The point, furthermore, is that the dramatic account of Hamlet, Prince of Denmark, in hardly any feature resembles the historical account of Hamlet, Prince of Jutland; and that hereinafter is set forth the antique story of the latter Norse potentate. One presents here, in brief,—just as once did yet other sober-sided historians, for many hundred years before the birth of William Shakespeare, —"the tragedy of 'Hamlet,' with the part of the Prince of Denmark omitted."

Should you ask for precision, the true Prince of Denmark proves to be Wiglerus.

The temptation is rather Herculean, in this paragraph, to become pedantic concerning the Skjöldunga Saga and Saxo Grammaticus and Niel of Sorö and François de Belleforest; to quote, at proper length, from the Wigleksaga; to mention (with a suitable feint of familiarity) the folk-tale of Brjam, and the prose Edda, and the Annals of the Four Masters; and to dwell, if only in passing, upon the Ambales Saga and the Hrolfsaga Kraba: so that I might tell you, thus tediously, how the more ancient Scandinavian writers dealt with Hamlet of Jutland. I avoid this temptation. I say merely that the story of his exploits and of his ending exists in variant versions, each one of which agrees with the other versions as concerns the general outline of events, but differs widely as to details of action and as to the minor characters involved.

Hereinafter it has seemed best to follow the special version which was current, in English, during the lifetime of Shakespeare, or of whoever did contrive the stage-story of Hamlet. This account was translated, from out of the French, in all probability not long after 1570; it appears to have been the immediate source of the play: in any case, it must have been used—though, possibly, in its original French form—by the playwright (whether or not he was Shakespeare) who before 1589 had turned the historical Hamlet of Jutland into the fictitious "Hamlet of Denmark"; and who first foisted, for dramatic purposes, into this revamped ancient story the unquiet and magniloquent ghost of Hamlet *père*. No one of Hamlet's earlier biographers knew of any such phantom. Yet furthermore, this same history must have been consulted by Shakespeare when, about the year 1600, he fashioned the play we now possess.

For these reasons I have preferred the text of this special version, where it differed from yet other versions, in any matter of detail. As a chronicle of Norse life during the first decade of the eighth century, it displays a few anachronisms which (in view of their unimportance) I have left uncorrected; and it may or it may not be the most truthful account of Hamlet of Jutland which now survives; but that it is the most important account of him which ever existed could be denied only by the incurably earnest-minded—such as invest faith seriously in the plenary inspiration of literature by life,—inasmuch as this account gave, directly, to the supreme English poet the materials of his conceded masterpiece. One edits it reverently and with circumspection.

Yet, some incidents, along with a vast deal of the declamatory *tirades* and the long-winded moralizing of the old story, have been abridged. Its more candid improprieties have been palliated or

softened. Its notably vague handling of geography
has been redressed with the aid of the Wigleksaga,
in preference to the odd variations of Saxo Grammaticus,—so that (to cite but one example) I have
honored veracity by permitting Fengon to perish,
as in the Wigleksaga he did perish, at Sundby
rather than at Viborg. I have stricken out, as im-
material, any mention of the King of Deira's ple-
beian-born sixth wife. And in a few passages, where
such ellipses were met with as left matters either
unsufficingly explained or not explained at all, I
have made the additions which were suggested, not
by imagination, but by an equally illustrious exile
from American letters, called human nature.

The relation between Fengon and Hamlet, for
instance, I have viewed in the light of biological
facts very plainly stated even by Shakespeare; to
the battling between Hamlet and his father-in-law
I have given, at worst, a lucidity absent from the
original ancient story; whereas the part which is
played by Wiglerus has been supplemented, rather
liberally, from his own saga,—a narrative that, in
all likelihood, stayed unknown to the dramatists of
Elizabeth's England.

One grants that in the Wigleksaga he is called
Wiglek, just as Fengon appears therein as Feng,
and Fengon's murdered brother as Horwendill, and
Hamlet as Amleth, but—except only as concerns
the too weighty nominal error of calling Rörek

Slyngebond "King Roderick"—I have thought it preferable to keep the Tudorian form of all proper names, in order that the old, famous, misinterpreted story (so far as it involves Hamlet) might come to you, in its every essential, as Shakespeare first found it. I may dare assert, at least, that I have not changed the story quite so improbably or constantly, or so grandly, as he did.

Poynton Lodge
July 1939

PRINCIPAL CHARACTERS

DANES

RÖREK SLYNGEBOND ....King of the Danes
EINAR ⎫
THORFIN ⎬ his three sons
WIGLERUS ⎭
GERUTH, his daughter, married first to Horvendile, and afterward to Fengon

JUTLANDERS

GERVENDILE CUT-THROAT, King of Jutland, then a province of Denmark
HORVENDILE ⎱ his two sons, the successive husbands
FENGON ⎰ of Geruth
HAMLET ....son to Geruth
ORTON ....friend to Hamlet
CORAMBUS ....a privy counsellor
INGRID ....his daughter
THORA FAIR-SKIN, second wife to Earl Sigmund of Lökken

BRITONS

EDRIC ....King of the Deiri, Fengon's foster-brother
GUDRUN ....the mother of Edric

PRINCIPAL CHARACTERS

ALFTRUDA .... daughter to Edric
SIWARD SWIFT-FOOT .... an outlaw

SCOTS

HERMETRUDE .... Queen of Pictland
ESTRILD .... her sister
FERBIS, the Lord of Ablach, in love with Hermetrude
MAGNUS THE SKALD .... an executioner
A DWELLER AMONG TOMBS

CONTENTS

CONTENTS

HAMLET HAD AN UNCLE

"Of carnal, bloody and unnatural acts,
Of accidental judgments, casual slaughters."

1

THE SKIN OF SIGMUND'S WIFE: HOW IT GOT HORVENDILE OUT OF HIS KINGDOM

IN JUTLAND AT THIS TIME LIVED DOZENS OF women who were no less beautiful than the wife of Earl Sigmund óf Lökken, but none who had a more superb complexion. She was called, for this reason, Thora Fairskin; and among her admirers was Prince Wiglerus, the King of Denmark's third son.

This admiration was natural enough, because Wiglerus (who had just come out of Ragwak, after evading the not unjustified malice of the Sultan of Alcore) was by way of being a virtuoso of the beauties of women. Now Wiglerus, so far as he knew, was not actually in love with Thora Fairskin; but he did get an æsthetic delight from looking at her. Her features were good, her hair commendable, her eyes pleasing, her hands excellent: and her skin was marvellous. When you said gallant things to her, then all her small soft face became colored tenderly, like an illumination in honor of your eloquence, of your arch wit, and perhaps even

[3]

of your seductiveness. To an unattached well-seasoned adventurer who, at the instant, did not have in progress any affair of the heart, this spectacle was agreeable. That was all, at least for the present.

Meanwhile, Prince Wiglerus enjoyed this innocent sort of but partly earnest love-making; and through his indulgence in it, he induced far-reaching results, because if, upon the afternoon which begins this story, Wiglerus had not paused in the corridor, to exchange amenities with Thora Fairskin, then Wiglerus would have accompanied his brother-in-law Horvendile into the bedroom of Horvendile's wife. There would, in that case, have been no murder.

As the affair fell out, during those affable moments which Wiglerus gave over to polite compliments, Horvendile was killed very hastily by his brother Fengon. Wiglerus, entering the bedchamber, thus found his sister Geruth to be unmistakably Horvendile's widow; and to the farther end of the room, at the bottom of an elaborately embroidered piece of tapestry which presented the last hours of the last Nibelungs, he found also Fengon arising from a hurried inspection of the corpse of Horvendile.

Fengon smiled, somewhat sadly.

"My poor brother would have killed both

Geruth and me," said Fengon. "But he had a weakness for the more obvious platitudes. So by good luck he paused first to denounce us suitably. By still better luck, I struck him, suitably, before his sword was out."

Then said Geruth, who even in her present state of undress retained her strong sense of decorum,—

"Yet it was not the part of a brave warrior to strike him from behind, my darling."

"Nor was it the act of an intelligent person, my dearest, to turn his back upon me to rebuke you as a detected adulteress," replied Fengon.

Wiglerus spoke next, in tones which he kept carefully neutral.

"So Horvendile, at long last, has caught the two of you in bed together. As a result, we confront a corpse with a hole in its back. That is awkward. There is no Demosthenes who could convince an idiot that Horvendile tried to run away from Fengon. Through this hole must leak out some unavoidable scandal. We must make the best of it."

The Prince of Denmark reflected for an instant.

"Now then, Fengon, do you finish dressing! and do me the kindness to remember you found Horvendile about to kill Geruth. You struck in order to save her. By good luck he was tipsy. Put straight the bedcovers, Fengon, if you please. Stand quiet, my sister. This will not hurt you, not very much, and this is eminently necessary."

Wiglerus drew out the dead man's sword from its scabbard. He struck swiftly, but with neat precision, making a long shallow cut in Geruth's left arm, which bled freely. He put the bloodied sword in dead Horvendile's right hand.

"So," says Wiglerus, "our evidence is prepared. You may scream now, my sister."

All three of them shouted for aid.

2

THE TWO SONS OF GERVENDILE CUT-THROAT

PEOPLE TALKED, OF COURSE, AS TO THIS FRATRICIDE in the reigning family of Jutland, but all persons of responsibility applauded Fengon. His honesty no less than his anguish was evident; for Fengon had loved his dead brother: that was known, even by his own admission. Few other persons, excepting gentlewomen whose tenderness was to be rented on a commercial basis, had loved this overbearing, boisterous, dissolute Horvendile; and the Jutlanders upon the whole were content to be rid of him. If in his drunken frenzy he had succeeded in murdering the King of Denmark's daughter (that noble lady whom demonstrably he had already wounded), why, then, it was obvious, Denmark would have punished all small Jutland. In protecting Geruth, heroic Fengon had protected also his people. Such was the applausive verdict of the subjects of Fengon, who now reigned alone.

Before this time, he and his brother Horvendile had ruled jointly over the province of Jutland.

They were sons to that Gervendile (called rightly the Cut-Throat) who in his own day had been King of Jutland up to the hour of his death by burning. His overlord, the King of Denmark, had then given Jutland to the valiant and warlike heirs of his deceased servitor; and both of them had since proved noble Vikings, who killed and plundered their adversaries with distinction. So the two Kings of Jutland got praise which they well deserved. Even though they showed at their supreme best in piracy, because of their more constant practice of this art, yet in no form of marauding or of high-handed assault did they at any time fall short of a spirited rendition. Fengon, it was granted, displayed the more finesse in entrapping the foe; Fengon fought subtly, through small steady demolitions, so that many of his rivals declared some of Fengon's most excellent work to be lacking in gusto: but the buccaneering of Horvendile was in an heroic style which not even the unfriendly could shrug away as merely grandiose. Horvendile attacked any and all opponents with the bright candor of a thunderbolt; and got very much the same results, usually.

Thus it was Horvendile who, in a most tremendous battle, which was talked about in the north parts of the world for weeks, and became the subject of four drapas (as the Norse called their heroic poems), had defeated and killed King Collere of Norway, and pillaged the King's fleet of inordinate riches. Horvendile killed moreover at this time, after ravishing her in public, on the foredeck of her own ship, the King's sister Svafa, who was considered the best warrior of her day. In that day many women followed the profession of arms. Of the treasures which Horvendile fetched home from these glorious doings, he of his own accord sent one-third to his liege-lord, Rörek Slyngebond; and the pleased King of Denmark, in fair exchange, brought his fair daughter Geruth into Jutland and there married her to Horvendile.

Horvendile liked Geruth well enough: but gallant Fengon worshipped his sister-in-law from the first instant he saw her. He confessed as much to her, because candor is a virtue becoming to nobly born persons. As a gentlewoman of refined taste, she could not help but prefer the sincere and courteous love-making of Fengon to the rough ways of Horvendile; as a kind-hearted person, she could not but pity the distressful condition of Fengon. So the inevitable followed. They sinned, technically at all events, no great while after Geruth's marriage; and if they continued sinning, the affair was managed with discretion, and to their finding, nobody was a penny the worse for it. Certainly Horvendile did not suffer because of their mutual affection; for that loud-mouthed brusque fighting-man, having got a son to succeed him, had nowadays the leisure for such broad-minded ladies as entertained him in bedchambers far more lively than he had ever shared with Geruth.

Fengon alone was not wholly happy during these years of deceit and adultery. He loved Geruth with entire faithfulness. But he loved likewise, or at any rate he intensely admired, his elder brother, that fine strong splendid animal who got so much zest out of life. Time and again kind-hearted Fengon had put aside the idea of bewitching or of poisoning his brother, as well as the more noble notion of securing Horvendile's happiness in Valhalla with a battle-ax or a knife-thrust, because although one or the other of these sedatives was the plainly sensible remedy, yet fraternal affection found every one of them to be repugnant.

It was dangerous to let Horvendile live. Such unwise clemency involved a daily discomfort and continual subterfuges which the native frankness of Fengon abhorred. Yet so unbounded was his brotherly love that he did not ever dispose of Horvendile until accident had compelled Fengon to do this, out-of-hand, in mere self-protection. The huge, bull-headed, stupid, wholly dear creature had blundered in upon Geruth and Fengon in circumstances which could not possibly have been explained away. Fengon had thus either to kill or to be killed instantly; and but for the adroit aid and the convenient testimony of Prince Wiglerus, affairs might have turned out badly.

Wiglerus meantime was yet further enforced by his moral duty to protect the credit of his sister and of his family at large. He said farewell to Thora Fairskin with gallant regret; and then journeyed toward Elsinore, where he told his father, King Rörek Slyngebond, as much about the manner of Horvendile's death as seemed advisable.

3

OF GERUTH AND HER SECOND HUSBAND

"IN BRIEF, MY DEAR GERUTH," SAYS FENGON, "Wiglerus has been at large pains to settle this somewhat disagreeable affair. He has represented the matter to your father in a proper light, through the aid of some unavoidable perjury. And his wise suggestion that, for the sake of Jutland, you and I should be married at once, was introduced to my counsellors with your brother's unfailing tact. We should always be grateful to Wiglerus."

"It is really a comfort to be married to you," Geruth admitted, "because it makes me feel far more respectable than to be meeting you in that hole-and-corner way which I never did quite enjoy, with somebody apt to pop in at almost any moment."

"Yet for me to marry you, my dear, was an extremity of fortune-hunting," returned Fengon, smiling. "A marriage between us two—just as wise Wiglerus pointed out to the council—was the most politic manner of keeping me, no less than all my loyal counsellors, in office now and forever, by

[12]

making sure that your father would continue my appointment as King of Jutland. Wiglerus thinks of everything off-hand. It is a rare trait; and I would that I shared it."

Very lightly Geruth touched her husband's left ear as she passed him, going toward her embroidery frame.

"You are too tender-hearted, Fengon," she observed, as she took up her bag of silks; "and I always said so. If only you had not been so very foolishly tender-hearted about Horvendile, for example, and so pig-headed too about taking my advice, then we could have been rid of him years ago."

"But I loved my big blustering foolish brother," said Fengon fondly; "and even nowadays, although everything has ended quite happily, like an old fairy tale, it troubles me, once in a while, to remember that, of all Vikings, I should have been the person to ensure his eternal welfare, perhaps a tiny bit roughly."

The Queen answered: "My dearest, that is wholly sweet of you; and I can quite see your point of view. I do not share it, of course. I was not Horvendile's brother, but only his wife. Yes, and I was married to him the first day I ever saw him, without being consulted in the matter one way or the other, and I never pretended to love him, any more than he did me. Yet I do not bear him any least ill-will; and so it is a sound comfort to me to know that he is now in Valhalla, with any number of Valkyries about, who will not mind his coming to bed with them drunk every night, as I did mind extremely. There would be no earthly sense in saying I did not."

"Yes, but," says Fengon, "we ought to feel remorse."

"I do feel remorse," replied Geruth. "It is not at all pleasant to remember that I lived in a state of sin for so long. Yet I must remind you, my darling, that it was wholly your fault, because if only you had taken my advice, poor Horvendile would have inherited eternal bliss a long while before he did; and our wickedness would not have been anything like so extensive."

"Still," Fengon pursued, "I assisted him out of the toils and disappointments of human life; and in consequence I ought to be horror-stricken. I ought to be entirely miserable."

"You defended yourself against an enraged bellowing bull, who was about to murder you, and me also, my dear Fengon; and in mere point of fact you are not a bit miserable, except when your stomach is upset. You ought not to have touched that bacon this morning. And I told you so at the time."

Fengon replied: "My dearest, I have loved you since the first moment I saw you. So I admit it is not possible for me to be unhappy, or even suitably remorseful, now that I have you all to myself. I have taken some of the tonic."

"Why, then all is as it should be, my dear husband; and we need have no further worries to bother us. Except of course fried food of any kind, which you really ought to be more careful about."

"And except Hamlet," says Fengon.

"The affliction of our unlucky son," replied Geruth piously, "is the will of Heaven. We can but make the best of it."

Having thus put the matter in divine hands, she turned her own capable hands toward her temporarily put-by needlework; and averted, tranquilly, from unremunerative regret to some much needed embroidery. Fengon regarded her with fond admiration.

She is very wonderful, thought Fengon, and I am not worthy to possess a helpmate so matter-of-fact, so sensible, and so brave. Not even to me will she admit in full her sorrow as to young Hamlet's mental condition. Instead, she does make the best of it, a trifle sanctimoniously perhaps, but with sound resignation; and to every appearance her concern about the poor lad is less deep than mine.

Perhaps, Fengon meditated yet further, the

union which existed between Geruth and himself was so firm-set, and had been buttressed so stoutly by the tranquil years of their incest, as to make both of these lovers a thought callous toward other persons. Fengon recalled that, during the progress of their secret romance, he had felt upon many occasions that Geruth really ought to be somewhat more remorseful over her betrayal and her systematic hoodwinking of his brother. Fengon felt now that her affection for him subdued, or at least kept to the back of her mind, her maternal affection for Hamlet; and, with entire illogic, Fengon resented this. He wanted Geruth, his all-perfect wife, to be likewise an all-perfect mother.

That, however, was the trouble with all men who had once been idealists, and who, when youth left them, had put aside the high-hearted harum-scarum doings of youth, to live as they best might in a workaday flesh-and-blood world: they still hungered after, they even looked for, the noble absurdities in which they no longer believed. Once, when young Fengon and young Wiglerus and young Edric had adventured no less happily in battles than between bed-covers, and when the three of them had bustled about half the known world as gay soldiers of fortune, then you had found everywhere divinely beautiful and witty and philanthropic female creatures of whom to-day's women, even at their best, appeared to be uninspired copies. You loved Geruth with entire affection; the special sort of excitement with which you had once regarded her had given way, perhaps, to a sort of but half amused impatience: yet you would not willingly have your prosaic dear wife changed in any least particular. It was merely that you remembered, even nowadays, the more flawless and the finer sweethearts whom you had known when everybody was young. You felt, somehow, that your loyal and complete satisfaction with Geruth, and with your lot in general, was a betrayal of that young Fengon who to-day did not exist anywhere.

Instead, a graying Fengon, with his hair thinning and with his digestion become a more or less ever-present consideration, sat here in contentment, by and large, with his plump wife and his well-furnished castle and his thriving province. Yonder in Britain, as King of the Deiri, an ageing but still red-headed Edric was equally pre-occupied, and equally satisfied, no doubt—or at any rate almost satisfied, just as you were,—by the amusing puzzles of statecraft, and by the bracing outdoor exercise of an occasional war, and by a reigning monarch's official employments in general. Dapper Wiglerus alone of the three comrades (under a thatching of sleek brown hair, which the rascal quite probably dyed) still went about his wanderings pretty much as he elected, inasmuch as Wiglerus, being only the third son of the King of Denmark, stayed unencumbered by any special duties.

Yet Wiglerus, no matter with what gay firmness he defied time and its ugly dilapidations, no longer was young. Nobody anywhere whom you had once known and loved, or whom you had hated, with a vigor now strange to you, was young any longer. Life would not ever be any more lofty in confidence, or in possibilities, than it was to-day; there could be for you no more rapture, no more beguiling hope that, by-and-by, your existence would become resplendent and wholly satisfying, somehow, and would continue a display of such characteristics forever. You could hope, now, at best, for a continuance of but slowly aggravated infirmities, and for a relatively unpainful death— at no remote date. It was not youth which you missed, but the eternally deluded hopefulness and the impermanent bright sheen of youth's lost world.

"See now," says Fengon, to himself, "but how insatiable is the greed of a romanticist, even when, by every romantic tradition, his lot turns out to be the most happy imaginable! All ends like an old fairy tale, with virtue attaining to its just reward, and with true love winning its desired recompense. I have won my kingdom; I am married to that special princess whom I loved and whom I still prefer above all other women; I possess wealth and comfort; and in the bright sunset of living, I may now, with all common-sense to back me, look forward to an extended season of political and domestic happiness. Yet I am not really content; for the illness of Hamlet is to me a perpetual small worry."

Thus Fengon meditated, while his plump handsome Geruth nodded over her embroidery, and each one of them thought about Hamlet.

4

OF HAMLET: HOW HE TROUBLED PEOPLE

HAMLET WAS THAT SON WHOM THE LOVING EN-
deavors of Geruth and Fengon had begotten in the
bed of Horvendile. They tell of yellow-haired big
Hamlet how inexpressibly was his conduct adapted
to distress his parents. Almost daily he would fall
into shocking seizures of epilepsy, during which he
stripped many of the clothes from his body, and
rolled about wherever he had tumbled down, with
his tongue protruding from his mouth and bleeding
where he had bitten his tongue. Arising, he would
run about at random in the King's palace, or
through the streets, as silent and unswerving as a
mad dog.

Upon yet other occasions he would seem to
talk fluently: there was no stopping him then, nor
could you find in his talk any consecutive meaning.
It was a mere torrent of phrases, surging and
jostling and swirling endlessly, while he stamped
about, scratching and digging at the ground with

his feet and flapping his arms, as if they had been wings, and pausing only to crow like a cock, to grunt like a hog, or perhaps to bellow like an enraged cow. At other times he would speak curtly, with an abrupt surliness, but even then he spoke incomprehensibly. There was no end to the perturbing antics of young Hamlet.

Thus Fengon finds him standing at the fireside sharpening a stick of kindling wood with a small black-horn-handled knife.

"What play is this, my dear son?" says Fengon.

Hamlet bleated as a sheep bleats. He said afterward:

"I make ready for the future. I prepare sharp darts and piercing arrows to revenge the death of brave Horvendile."

This was not pleasant talk, and quiet-spoken Fengon showed his disapproval of it.

"Come, Hamlet, but let us be sensible! That I found it my duty, and indeed my highly distressing duty, to put my beloved brother out of living, is granted; it is granted freely; and your thankfulness to me for that act of self-denial ought to be extreme, inasmuch as I thus preserved your dear mother's life."

"So it is reported, my lord King."

"Should you but have the kindness, Hamlet,

not to interrupt me, we would reach far more quickly, I believe, a mutual understanding."

Fengon then spoke, for about three minutes, in his best public manner, concerning the omniscience, the material utility, the incessantness, the depth, and a few other unparalleled traits of maternal affection; but he concluded by saying:

"Moreover, Hamlet, I am a sea-robber of some little distinction. In my time I have sacked Gimsar and Varness and Medalhus and Skirding. I have sailed my own ship into battle upon twenty-seven occasions, with but two defeats. And so—without mentioning any names whatever, my dear son,— I say only that for anybody to be planning to kill me with a stick of kindling wood, quite apart from the ingratitude and the wickedness of any such notion, appears disrespectful. It is unbecoming."

Hamlet answered, with a frown and scraping his absurd slight sticks one against the other:

"It is yet more unbecoming, my lord King, that Horvendile, who feared nobody, should have died from a wound in his back. The wounds of the brave dead are, by ordinary, to the front of the corpse."

Very patiently Fengon explained, still again, to this scowling tall boy, that Fengon had struck from behind because there was no other manner in which to save the life of Geruth.

"My poor brother had already wounded her, Hamlet, as the world knows. His second blow would have ended all; and his dripping sword was raised to deliver that blow. It was an appalling sight. My blood chills when I remember it. So I struck first. I had no choice."

"And I, too," says Hamlet, "I have no choice."

His eyes, which for the moment had been steadfast and coolly appraising, shifted away from the compassionate and cordial glance of Fengon. Hamlet began to stamp about the room, flapping his arms, with his big hands clenched tightly.

"I am haunted!" says Hamlet. "There are too many whisperings at Sundby. You are friendly and honor-loving. There is no malice in you. Your good fame and your conscience are spotless. They are like the clean cool sheets which a thriving harlot makes ready against the night's traffic. That night rises. Fiends whisper in its twilight, gray limping fiends who prompt me with strange advice. They are most impudent fiends, to be talking scandal about King Fengon."

With that pious vagueness which a majority of fathers find to be advisable when instructing their children as to continence, the King answered:

"No middle-aged sea-robber, my dear son, is immune from slander; nor is even a budding pirate safe from the evil suggestions of hell. We can but pray to Odin to defend us."

Yet Fengon was troubled. He knew hatred when he saw it. And it was hatred which, for one calm moment, had looked down at him through the gray-blue eyes of his tall son.

5

INGRID GOES INTO THE WOODS

"I am not sure," says Fengon, "whether my dear son be insane or, more simply, intractable. I do not know what he plans. But I do know he distrusts his own father. That is not as it should be. That indeed is a situation which wrings my heart. It wrings my heart unendurably. For the boy's own good, I must get his confidence."

Grieved Fengon sent for Corambus of Elling, so as to confer with that learned counsellor; and Corambus, in turn, conferred with the daughter of Corambus. This noble maiden was called Ingrid; and if some persons carpingly debated her chastity, none questioned her beauty or her intelligence. The latter prompted her to make the most of the former. She did.

She assented, with a proper filial deference, to the task of gaining young Hamlet's confidence; and she thus met the Prince—by the most astounding sort of coincidence, to which the lovely blonde girl could not deny its fit tribute of vocal wonder—just

after Hamlet had parted from a lame gray gentleman in the wood of Sundby.

Ingrid, however,—let it be explained in de-
fence of her moral principles,—had not any need to
trouble her fair head as to the propriety of her being alone in this forest. She well knew that, behind
an elm-tree, her learned father squatted in watchful
attendance, so that he might report to King Fengon
as to the doings and words of Hamlet. And Corambus did as much, in due course.

The dear child (reported Corambus) spoke
with that frankness which one might expect in an
always dutiful daughter. She confessed that for
weeks she had regarded Hamlet with a pure and
unbounded affection; she trusted he would not look
upon her candor as unmaidenly, but would continue to respect the integrity of her intentions and
the purity of her past life thitherto, even in case of
an outcome which she was too modest to put into
words, but illuminated with a fond blush; she re-
ferred with enthusiasm to his manly beauty, to the
rare charm of his conversation, and to his intimi-
dating nobility in quarters which to Corambus, in
his concealment, remained invisible; she mentioned
the circumstance that upon this bank of soft cool
moss, which was really not unlike a bed, they were

quite alone, with nobody within miles of them, even were she to scream for aid never so loudly; and she suggested, in brief, through every possible polite provocative, that not merely her affections were at Hamlet's disposal.

Hamlet sighed; and the surprised girl asked the cause of his sorrow in a situation so highly agreeable.

Says Hamlet: "I grieve because I must compel my heart to listen to my head. You are a charming person with whom it would be a pleasure to cast prudence to the winds. I am cordially pleased that you should find me to be heroic and attractive and —as I believe you mentioned likewise—quick-witted and entertaining, in an unexampled degree. Hah, but no one, you must let me assure you, my dear Ingrid, shall ever know about your infatuation except only ourselves."

"Why, then—" says Ingrid.

"For the rest, I am still young," Hamlet continued, with a becoming diffidence. "As I advance in life, I shall meet other ladies, who may admire me equally on account of my heroism and attractiveness and quick wits. When I have come to be wooed by these other gentlewomen, with honorable intentions and under the sanction of propriety, and when I have had a chance to perceive how strong is the fascination I exert over all these gentlewomen,

then I may be wholly glad I have no illicit past
under these bushes to bring out sorrowfully into
the open. It might grieve a large number of these
fond gentlewomen. I owe it to them to consider in
due season their natural anguish. I ought to fore-
stall their anguish."

"But—" Ingrid said.

"And besides that," Hamlet went on, with a
continuing air of reflection, "immoral conduct very
often assumes a serious aspect, should the offence
become generally known. No matter how cautious
and respectable a young man may be, there is no
way of telling whether or not the woman with
whom he strays into folly will protect his good
name. Beautiful blonde women, in particular, cannot ever know the value of discreet speech. How
can they well esteem reticence, with so little experience of it as they enjoy, do these beautiful blonde
women with whom no man upon the livelier side of
his dotage is able to talk sanely?"

"Still—" said Ingrid.

"Nor should we fail to weigh the possibility of
a yet darker outcome," Hamlet resumed. "Many a
fine young man through one moment's unwisdom
has found himself unbuttoned into fatherhood and
a compulsion of marriage and the curtailing of his
liberty. He has been misled, by unbridled passion,
into years of self-respect and thrift and praise-

worthy behavior, at a time when he would prefer to be dissolute and to enjoy life. Is not the small heart-ache which I feel just now, in preserving my personal purity, to be chosen rather than any of these harsh possibilities? I think so; and I think too, dear Ingrid, that I shall not wring your neck—at all events, not this morning."

Ingrid said, "Hah!"

Hamlet answered her: "I may be wrong in believing that a young man, among such idyllic surroundings, may do well to preserve his virtue rather than to put faith in a sleek lying cuddling bitch. Yet I do not think I am wrong when I consider the many insects which infest elm-trees. And this thesis I stand ready to argue against all persons, no matter how learned they may be—even against Socrates and Solomon and Corambus of Elling,—that a judicious nephew ought now and then to compel his heart to listen to his head."

Then Hamlet began to crow like a cock; and he ran away from fair Ingrid, laughing madly, and bellowing, and grunting, and squealing also, in an unbecoming fashion.

All this did Corambus report; and he added that, howsoever gratifying one of course found it to hear oneself associated with the leading sages of

Greece and Judea, one could not but regret Prince Hamlet's backwardness in chivalry.

"—For to what," says Corambus, "is the younger generation coming, when even in the presence of an unprotected fond girl a young man can thus openly talk about his own personal purity, and maintain it too, without shame? Matters were not like this in the better times of our youth, my lord King, when at all costs the needs of a gentlewoman were honored."

"You speak truth, my wise counsellor," returned Fengon, "and the world worsens. Yet in my opinion, Hamlet also has found some counsellor or another. He did not voice the native sentiments of a descendant of Gervendile Cut-Throat; nor are these well rounded periods in the manner of Hamlet's blunt jerky way of speaking. I would very much like to know more about that lame gray person of whom your daughter had a glimpse. Meanwhile, we must endeavor, through some other agency, to gain the boy's confidence."

6

CONTINUED MISADVENTURE IN GERUTH'S BEDROOM

"WELL, BUT AFTER ALL," SAYS FENGON, "IT IS IN his mother, alone of women, that a young man may confide utterly so long as he does not know any better."

The next morning, when day broke, and the chamberlains came to serve King Fengon, they equipped him with a green hunting coat and tight fitting boots. His gilt spurs were fastened on; he mounted his racing steed, he hung his horn about his neck, and he seized in his hand his boar spear, now that the King of Jutland made ready to hunt in the forest of Sundby attended by his earls, his hunters, and ten traces of dogs.

At this time Corambus went into the bed-chamber of Geruth, so that he might report to King Fengon as to the doings and words of Hamlet. The Queen hid Corambus of Elling behind the tapestry at the foot of which Horvendile had found death; and upon which were represented, in lively colors, the still more picturesque departures, from out of human flesh toward heavenly judgment, of Högni the Brave and of King Gunnar.

Geruth sent for Hamlet. He came clucking and crowing and scratching at the ground with his feet.

"My son," says the Queen, "such conduct disturbs me. It is calculated to provoke remark. It compels me to point out you are not in a chicken run."

Hamlet answered that by quacking and hissing like an incensed gander; then he began to bray, and to moo, and to bleat, and to whinny.

"—Nor a barn, either," the Queen returned. "I do wish you would not be so silly."

"Bow-wow," says Hamlet, sniffing at the tapestry by the doorway and lifting up his left leg.

"—Although of course, my dear boy, if it does at all amuse you to play at being a chicken or a dog or anything of that kind, why, a large number of young men do spend their spare time a great deal more viciously. That much I would be the very last person in the world to deny."

Hamlet said, "Miaow," as he leaped about the room, scratching at the tapestries, first here, then there, with his finger-nails. He thus felt the body of Corambus behind the tapestry at the farther end of the apartment.

"A rat, Grimalkin! poor Tybalt has caught a rat!" cried Hamlet, as he whipped out his sword.

He grasped the hilt of it with both hands, and he so dug with the point of his heavy sword into the tapestry.

Corambus screamed. But Hamlet, still miaowing and spitting like an enraged cat, pulled out the old quaking wounded man into the open. In front of the tapestry which represented the last hours of the last Nibelungs, and in precisely the same place where Fengon had aided Horvendile's going up into Valhalla, the Prince murdered Corambus.

Hamlet removed the body, and he disposed of it in a fashion which was afterward criticized more or less unfavorably. The Prince returned to speak with his mother; and in regard to this speaking (so the tale tells) Geruth was not utterly candid with Fengon, later on, when a little after sunset the King came back from his day's outing in the forest of Sundby.

7

NOW CORAMBUS BEGINS A BLOOD-FEUD

"Poor Hamlet talked his usual sort of wild nonsense," Geruth told the King of Jutland. "He continued to behave like a barnyard; and I humored him as I best might. It does not matter, one way or the other, whether he mooed or bleated. He crows rather well, though. Did you have a nice hunt? All boys are more or less flighty; but they get over it by-and-by."

Fengon regarded the dear fluttered woman tenderly; and he said:

"My darling, I respect your position. You prefer neither to betray him to me nor me to him. That is as it should be, Geruth; and I honor this reticence, which befits equally the fond mother of Hamlet and the true-hearted wife of Fengon."

"But now, Fengon, now you quite misunderstand me—"

"To the contrary, so great is my affection for my adored wife and for my dear son that I understand, and applaud, both of you. For the boy has

intelligence," says Fengon, with paternal pride,
"and because of it he has set about deluding and
killing me in a wholly rational manner. Hamlet intends, at all costs, to get vengeance for his father's
death."

"Fengon, you are talking nonsense. Horvendile
was only Hamlet's uncle at utmost, although in a
manner of speaking, of course, he was his stepfather
too. But at any rate, you are his father—"

"Yes, my dearest; and I make bold to think it
is that fact which accounts for his intelligence; but
Hamlet does not know it. He reasons only that by
pretending to be insane he can preserve his own life
until he has found a good opportunity of taking
mine. It is not easy for a mere boy to kill unaided a
king in the publicity of court life; poor Hamlet
must bide his time; and I think he has contrived
the best possible device."

"Now, Fengon, if you would but let me explain—"

Fengon answered with a tolerant smiling:
"You must permit me to quote; and if I appear
somewhat highflown, that is, in the speech of youth,
a fault not unfamiliar. 'My mother, I put my trust
in you. I beseech you, as you value your own flesh
and blood, not to betray me to the bland betrayer
of your body and of your good name. Though he
have never so many flattering courtiers to defend

him, yet will I bring dark-hearted Fengon to his death. I am bound in honor to requite his wicked killing of my father, brave Horvendile.' "

Geruth said blankly, "So you were listening!" She added, with large dignity,—

"I do not think it was at all honorable of you, Fengon, to be spying upon your own wife in that way, quite as if I did not intend to tell you everything at the first possible moment."

"My conduct," the King agreed, "in view of your unfailing candor, was most reprehensible. I apologize for it. Nevertheless, I did leave the hunt. I did return unobserved while our poor boy was disposing of our poor Corambus. I did take the place of Corambus, behind the tapestry. So there is really not any need for you to repeat any of Hamlet's heroic denunciations. I was honestly touched by them, Geruth. Our son has an excellent heart; and to a degree truly astounding, his vocabulary defies my credulity. Neither you nor Ingrid has he addressed in the normal voice of Hamlet. He has found, it is evident, some widely-read gray counsellor to prepare for him these noble speeches which display, so exactly, that untutored eloquence of the human heart which one encounters only in the more elaborately polished forms of literature. He evinces, in brief, intelligence as well as firm moral principles, such as reflect credit upon both his parents."

"That, Fengon, sounds very well, the way you put it. But you had no right to be eavesdropping. And never did I hear of a right-thinking Viking, who was taught, by his own dear mother, how to worship Odin properly, and how to take plunder from heathen people in the correct way, doing anything of the sort."

"Come now, my darling," the King pleaded, "but everything is quite as it should be! There is no least need for you thus to excite yourself, inasmuch as now we both understand the boy intends to make an end of me upon the first available chance, I can take proper care of myself. It should be to our parental fondness, I submit, a great consolation to find him only a murderer instead of a maniac; for the latter condition cannot always be remedied. So do you smile at me, my precious! and let us plan to get Hamlet out of these parts as quickly as may be managed."

"In fact," said the perturbed Queen, "a change of climate, or perhaps a sea-trip, some time this summer—"

"That is it," says Fengon. "A sea-trip! but not this summer."

Before the man's masculine unreason, Geruth remained patient, upon the most flagrant possible scale, but without for one moment pretending to condone any such nonsense. Instead, she explained aloofly:

"I do not at all see, Fengon, how you can say not this summer. It might be just the proper cure for his nervous condition. Indeed, now I think of it, I am sure it is. I know that my own father, whenever he took cold or felt run down, has always made it a fixed rule to invade Norway or Sweden, quite informally, of course, with not more than two or three long-ships, so that you can attack villages up the smaller rivers without running aground. Or once and in a while, Russia. He led a five-day cattle raid in the island of Bornholm, only last August, on account of a touch of sciatica. Very certainly, August comes in the summer. Nor do I mean that Hamlet has sciatica. I mean the principle of the thing. Because, Fengon, it cured him completely; and the fact that, at his age, my father still has two salt herrings and a half-gallon of beer for breakfast every day in the year does show you, I think, that he knows how to look after his health."

Fengon said: "Yes, my dearest: your father is wholly wonderful; he is almost worthy of his daughter. But Hamlet cannot wait until summer; for the situation is not so simple as you think. I must tell you Hamlet has not merely killed Corambus. He has hacked the corpse into fragments. In addition, he has boiled these fragments, in your man Grettir's soap pot, until the meat fell away from the bones; and the distressing results Hamlet has thrust at random into the various privies of the castle. It was quite a shock to me, just now, in my own apartments, to find the head of Corambus glaring up at me in frank disapproval of an intention from which I at once refrained."

So utterly aghast was Queen Geruth that, for the moment, she approached concision, through saying:

"Why, but, Fengon! I never heard of such a thing! and I really do think Hamlet is going too far, with such a nice, clean, tidy old gentleman!"

Fengon put aside his wife's shrillness with the aplomb of a well-seasoned husband; and soothingly pointed out:

"Still, you and I, Geruth, can understand that in improvising new funeral customs Hamlet has been trying to foster a name for eccentricity. Between ourselves, I dare grant that his methods are rather nicely adapted to serve his ends. So I do not blame him; to the contrary! I applaud his intelligence. But the family of the deceased are certain to be less broad-minded. There is no one of the five stalwart sons of Corambus but will consider this unconventional and dispersed sort of burial to be open to invidious comment. They are bound in honor, as his nearest of male kin, to declare a blood-feud. Yet, by good luck, before the beginning of a blood-feud, the law allows to any murderer, whether a man or a woman, five days in which to leave the kingdom—"

"But in winter time a murderer is allowed two weeks," says Geruth, discontentedly.

"You are quite right, my dear, as always"— was the reply of fond Fengon. "Only, I do not gather, at the middle of May, exactly what—well! whatever you may be talking about, my adored one,—has to do with anything else."

"It is only that in winter there would have been more time to see about his underwear, Fengon, and his shirts too. So I really do think it would have been far more convenient if only he had waited until, say, just the first of November, before killing Corambus. Corambus would not have objected at all, I am certain, because he was always so very considerate—"

"Yes, my darling: I meant merely that Hamlet would have to fight each one of the sons of Corambus, from Leif to Asmund, in the order of their age, should Hamlet remain in Jutland for six days longer. I shall therefore take your advice—"

"And I must say, Fengon, it is high time you did take my advice. It would have been better for everybody if only my advice had been listened to a little more often in this house, because, heaven knows, I was always frank in speaking for your own good, although there is no need to go into that now, with six suits of underwear at the very least to be got ready."

"You are quite right, my dear," says Fengon; "and at all times I have found your advice to be invaluable. I shall accordingly send Hamlet into Britain, to live there in safety, with my good foster-brother Edric, until the sons of poor Corambus have agreed to accept, in place of a series of duels with our poor son, a proper payment of weregild."

"Just what is the weregild for Corambus?" Geruth inquired provisionally: for she knew of course that weregild (as people called the indemnity which it was optional for the kin of a murdered person to accept from the murderer instead of starting a blood-feud) was fixed by the social ranking of the deceased; and thus varied to almost any degree.

Fengon pulled a long face.

"The rate of a privy counsellor," he admitted, "is twelve gold marks, or ninety-six aurar of silver. That the sum is large I cannot deny: yet the fond heart of a father is still larger; and paternal devotion does not haggle in the talons of the law, or even in the teeth of extortion."

Geruth answered this aphorism with a formula which was only too familiar to Fengon's hearing, inasmuch as at all times this vague but generous-natured lady employed this same formula before the prospect of spending some more money. In brief, Geruth answered—with a vast and a most noble air of altruism and of abstruse thinking, flavored never so slightly with reproof—that, even so, it would be a saving in the long run.

Fengon often wondered when this long run would begin, but he had been taught, by experience, how far wiser it was not to ask questions about the matter.

—And nobody (Geruth continued) could deny that; nor could anybody have been more sincerely fond of Corambus: she quite disapproved of any such conduct; but when Hamlet was your own child, it did make a difference. You could not argue about it; it was simply a fact all parents had to face; nor would any proper sort of parent—she added, with a frank gleam of proffered battle—so much as dream of taking any other attitude, at this special time of all others; and that much she felt it her plain duty to say.

Fengon replied, "Yes, my darling; you are wholly right."

So was it that, after three unhurried dissertations, concerning shirts, and what Corambus had said only last Thursday, and the comparative inexpensiveness of killing people of rather less preeminence, the Queen of Jutland agreed—by-and-by—to the wisdom of sending Hamlet into Britain; and of committing his safety to the King of Deira.

8

THE LETTER THAT FENGON WROTE IN HIS PERPLEXITY

WE MUST NOW SPEAK ABOUT THE EXTREME SOR-
row of Fengon during the while that he wrote the
letter which asked the King of Deira to have Hamlet disposed of, either with a sword or a spear or
a battle-ax (inasmuch as no person who died otherwise could enter into Valhalla), at the first instant
which fell in with the King of Deira's convenience.
Well! and Edric could attend to the matter at once,
because under a civil cloaking of obtuseness, both
Edric and Wiglerus knew that Hamlet was Fengon's son. Edric would quite understand that no
proper-minded father would be contriving the
death of his own son unless a step so unordinary
for paternal affection were highly urgent.

It was, nevertheless, an ironic circumstance—
Fengon reflected, as he folded up his letter and
afterward closed it with the seal of the King of
Jutland—that Hamlet should be doomed by precisely those traits which Fengon most heartily admired in him. The young man, it seemed, had fore-

[44]

thought and intelligence and a rare gift for acting; Fengon rejoiced, pardonably, to have begotten any offspring so accomplished. Even the boy's one error, in trusting his mother, was a venial offence in anybody so young; not until middle-age did you learn that no human being could be trusted with safety. Fengon thought proudly about what a first-rate king Hamlet might have made, and of the delight with which Fengon would have reared an heir so promising, if only a so dear indulgence had been permitted to dulcify his declining days. But the boy likewise had inherited that mild pertinacity which marked Fengon's own character: the boy had wholly resolved to murder Fengon; and murder Fengon he would, unless with a father's fondness seasoned never so slightly with firmness, you dissuaded Hamlet from committing the dreadful crime of parricide by the sole means in your power.

You might tell him the truth about his parentage? It was a notion to which Fengon, after weighing it, could not grant ponderability. If Hamlet were the son of dull-witted Horvendile, such would have been the obvious solution; the boy, like your loud-mouthed dear brother, could have been hoodwinked into believing whatever you told him; and so would have stayed harmless. But the son of Fengon, it appeared, had the intelligence of Fen-

gon; he would see, just as in the same ticklish circumstances Fengon himself would have seen, how
plain, and in fact how flagrant, was the intended
deceit. The shrewd hard-headed youngster would
pretend docilely to believe; and then, by-and-by,
at the first chance which offered, then Hamlet
would kill. So the truth here would be unconvinc-
ing, precisely because it was the truth. There was
no help for it. Fate was just as inevitably compelling Fengon to assist Hamlet into Valhalla as
fate had once bullied Fengon into raising Horvendile toward the same blessed estate.

It was all quite deplorable, and it seemed rather
unfair, the King of Jutland reflected,—this way in
which, through no fault of his, he was being forced
to part, one by one, with the persons most dear to
him. It was enough to depress anybody who by
nature had Fengon's affectionate and peace-loving
disposition. He was not in the least bit surprised
when, of a sudden, he hiccoughed, because continued worrying always did upset his digestion nowadays.

As you got on in life, your digestion became
a factor wholly unpredictable. Your physicians
talked very gravely, and they looked at you with
a low-minded air of reserving judgment, and of
exercising an impolite amount of tact: but what,
after all, did they ever do about it, except to give

you disgusting and quite inefficient drugs! So did it come about that, after the already considerable annoyance of having to contrive the death of your only son, now you would have once more to begin taking that unpleasant purple stuff before every meal. Such were the drawbacks incidental to possessing a kindly nature and a tender heart, in the hard matter-of-fact circumstances of modern civilization.

Fengon sighed resignedly. He sent for the Earls Haakon and Olaf, and he gave them instructions, along with his letter.

9

SAILING OF THE SEA-HAWK: HAMLET AND HIS MOTHER

IT IS RELATED HOW, AT FENGON'S ORDERS, THEY manned the Sea-Hawk. So was it with a suitable magnificence, which in some degree soothed his paternal regrets, that Fengon sent Hamlet toward death, because in all Jutland there was no ship more splendid than the Sea-Hawk.

The story says that this vessel, builded soundly out of oak and riveted with iron, was long and slender, with thirty benches for the rowers. Her sails were striped, crosswise, with blue and yellow; and upon each sail a scarlet dragon (since Queen Geruth was the daughter of a Harfaager) struggled and ramped aspiringly. The ship's prow was a rigid and more emaciated dragon, gilded and having large red eyes; the outward sides of the vessel were adorned handsomely with bands of red and of yellow ochre. Abaft, hung over the bulwarks of the Sea-Hawk the sixty shields of her rowers, each shield displaying its own bright design; they glittered in the sunlight; and from the slowly moving oars of the Sea-Hawk, now that, upon this superb forenoon, she turned southward from the harbor at Blokhus, the waters of Skagerrak splattered and dripped, with a pleasantly dispersed radiancy, sparkling like gems.

These drops of waters were as salty and as copious as the unavoidable tears of a bereaved father, Fengon reflected sadly. That fancy pleased him; yes, it was neat: but no simile could make cheerful, and no refinements of ornate rhetoric could ever hope to veil with the tinsels of æsthetic approval, the fact that aboard the Sea-Hawk sailed Fengon's only child going toward the supernal pleasures of Valhalla. Fengon hiccoughed; and then dried his eyes with a dignity which his sound knowledge of classical writers, as opposed to his experience of court life, had taught him to think suitable for a king in anguish.

Now the tale tells likewise that before leaving Jutland, Prince Hamlet spoke with his mother, of whom he made three requests. The first of these was that she should keep safe the sticks of kindling wood which he had sharpened. He required also that she should have the banquet hall of the castle hung with fresh tapestries nailed to the walls. And his third asking was that during the forenoon of his approaching birthday, if by this time he had not

returned into Jutland, she should cause to be celebrated his funeral.

"Some new tapestries would be an excellent
notion in that big wooden barn of a room out in
those bare fields, my dear poor son," the Queen
replied. "The whole place does want brightening
up, as I have been telling your father for heaven
only knows how long, because I might as well have
been talking to a bed post. But no, Hamlet, not a
funeral. In fact, I must have suggested it dozens
and dozens of times, along with two more fireplaces,
so that the gentlemen could get drunk in comfort
without actually freezing. Fengon is like all other
men and never does seem to understand the plain
need of such things. And the sticks, of course, will
be no special trouble, on the top shelf in the closet."

"Then, madam, all is settled—"

The Queen answered: "I must say I am glad
you agree with me about the tapestries, Hamlet,
because you mean rather plain red ones, I suppose,
with just a dignified amount of goldwork, nothing
gaudy. It would be, in fact, a saving in the long run.
But a funeral appears to me quite unnecessary. A
funeral would be a sheer waste of money, my dear
son,—and especially on your birthday—unless you
came to it. I do not see whatever could have put
such a morbid idea in your head, when we have
so much to be thankful for, after all, if one only

looks at matters in the right way. I mean, if you came to the funeral carried by your pall-bearers, just as we all have to do in the end."

Here the Queen paused, to sigh religiously.

Hamlet said, "Yet, madam, this is an idea which was put into my head by the wisest person whom I have known."

"Now but was it indeed! Poor dear Corambus!" said the Queen.

"No, madam; I did not mean Corambus."

"Nobody, Hamlet, ever had a finer mind in Jutland, or a more pleasant disposition either," the Queen stated reprovingly. "For that reason, my dear son, I really do feel compelled to say that while I believe in letting bygones be bygones, and not nagging at people forever, still, at the same time! You see, it is not as if your own mother did not understand the better side of your nature, Hamlet, but far otherwise. And that reminds me you have not as yet told me, my son, who is this other so very wise person."

"Why, but upon my word, madam, I do not know. Nor"—Hamlet added, a bit gloomily—"nor do I care to know."

So was it Orton came into the story.

10

OF ORTON: HIS APPEARANCE AND HIS ADVICE AT STRAITHKELD

ORTON WAS GRAY. YOU OBSERVED HIS GRAYNESS AS a sort of permeating unemphasis, and as an avoidance of the vivid so painstaking as to become in itself rather remarkable. He was gray, alike in his person and his clothing, even from his hair to his shoes, in very many shades of gray, which did not contrast with one another, but blended as softly as a drifting of fogs. After this soothing grayness, you noted his exceeding kindliness; and you knew that not any unwise deed or wicked action upon your part could ever unsettle Orton's good-will into a dislike of human frailty. You could trust Orton to see the very worst side of you with a lenientness which hardly if at all fell short of approval.

He was of no age in particular. He had the indefinite seeming of a hale person who had lived with discretion, but for the most part indoors, during the last forty or it might be the last seventy years. In effect, Orton was not noticeable in any way except for a slight lameness of his right leg. He walked, therefore, at all times, with the aid of an orange-wood cane, upon which, as if crawling up this cane, was carved a small crocodile tinted green; and gray Orton sat now upon a gray sand bank holding this cane upright between his gray knees, as he gazed upon Hamlet, consideringly, with a compassionate benevolence.

"—For your position, my dear Prince," Orton resumed, "is one of extreme delicacy. This letter, as you will observe, calls for your instant death when once you have reached the court of Deira; it is the business of the Earls Haakon and Olaf to see to it that you reach Deira without delay; and we thus confront a situation in which, I submit, you cannot afford idleness."

The two of them sat together upon the beach of Straithkeld, where the Sea-Hawk had been run ashore for the night, and between them lay Fengon's letter. This letter was now open; and over its contents young Hamlet frowned.

"I had expected mischief," says he. "Here is worse than mischief. Against ice-blooded malevolence there is no cure."

"You wrong the ingenuity of virtue at bay," replied Orton: "for I am certain it has occurred long ago, to a person of your adroit wits, that you might permit me to forge quite another letter,

which will call instead for the death of your annoying gaolers, Olaf and Haakon. You have thought
too, I make no doubt, about the ease with which
you could close up this second letter, most con-
vincingly, with the signet ring of dead Horvendile,
there on your thumb. The seal of the King of
Jutland, upon your ring, is the same as Fengon's
own seal."

The Prince had scooped up with half-folded
fingers a quantity of beach sand, which he now
spilled back on the beach. He watched the small
sliding trickle as if it were an affair of importance.

"That would be neat enough, Orton, so far
as it goes. But it would not explain my own presence in Britain."

"King Edric, my Prince," remarked Orton,
"has a daughter. She is marriageable."

"Come," says Hamlet, "but the two facts are
well thought of! Yes, one might ask also, in Fengon's damned name, that Edric should give me this
damned daughter to be my wife. That would account for all. But I may not fancy the young tit."

"In that event, my Prince, I refer you to the
fifty-fourth law of the Gulathing. 'If a man wishes
to separate from his wife, he shall declare himself
separated from her at a time when each of them
may hear the voice of the other in the presence of
witnesses.' Nothing could be more simple; it is the

most popular of all our laws among married men; and in fact, King Edric himself has thus dismissed two wives."

"Excellent!" cried Hamlet. "You have been a good friend to me, Orton."

"Here then, as a yet further proof of my friendship," said Orton, "is your letter."

He produced it, from out of his gray bosom. Hamlet read this letter, moving his lips to form each word, in the manner of one who did not read often. He stroked his chin, in a condition of mind which flavored gratitude with distrust, and relief with some doubtfulness.

"So, you had ready this letter, you gray sorcerer! And in all respects it is Fengon's own writing."

"As time goes on, hand in hand with industry," replied Orton, "one acquires these minor accomplishments. Let us speak of more important matters. For there still remains the further difficulty that, the more thanks to your gifted impersonation of so many birds and animals in Jutland, you are now granted to be insane everywhere. Edric will not welcome a madman as his son-in-law."

Hamlet answered, heavily humorous: "My lost wits have been happily recovered afloat in the North Sea. In Britain you will find me to be as conventional as anybody else."

But Orton shook his benevolent gray head, as he sat there nursing his cane of orange-wood.

"My Prince," he said pleadingly, "I am a romanticist who is not satisfied by the ordinary drab run of affairs. It was that trait indeed which caused my lameness, through a fall I had rather early in life. However! as a philanthropist, I have not ever lamented over-selfishly a mishap but for which the police and the clergy might to-day be out of employment. So let us humor my foible for the surprising, the picturesque, even for the pyrotechnic! Let us contrive this matter of your wits' recovery in a fashion more truly striking; and permit the seeming lunatic to stand revealed, of a sudden, as a subtle and omniscient person! That, to my judgment, would be far more worthy of Prince Hamlet than a tame downfall, from the high-hearted histrionics of insanity, into the humdrum tediousness of everyday common-sense."

"I admit," said Hamlet, still prodding with his thick stumpy hair-grown fingers in the gray sand, "what this letter well shows. For me to continue crowing and bleating and grunting, in the fashion of a village idiot, will not any longer protect me against Fengon. I admit also that I do not understand what you mean."

"I mean only, my dear Prince, to speak with you concerning the cornfields and the bacon and the drinking water, as well as the parentage, of King Edric."

—Whereafter Orton did speak of these matters. And handsome slow-witted Hamlet listened, with painstaking attention, biting at his fingernails, with his light-colored eyes narrowed. He said by-and-by:

"I see. But I do not see, Orton, why you should thus continually aid me without asking for any compact between us. Before to-day you have shown me how to pretend madness; and how to denounce Fengon, for my mother's benefit, most nobly. You have taught me with what kind of balderdash to check itching Ingrid from yet further pawings at me. You have promised me my desires—"

"Eh, but yes! for you desired merely to revenge Horvendile's death, and to become King of Jutland, and to leave behind you a name"—here Orton chuckled—"eternally famous. What are such trifles between princes?"

"You," Hamlet said, "I believe to be a prince of darkness."

"Now, my dear Prince, but in this enlightened age who puts faith in mere priestly fables? Would any demon be giving you, at no cost at all, such friendly advice as I have afforded? or be at pains to write out, for you to memorize, the exalted sentiments with which you have favored

Dame Ingrid and Dame Geruth? Even granting me to be some fiend or another, how need it matter to you who worship Odin?"

"Well—" Hamlet said conditionally.

"Upon the faith of a proverbially famous gentleman," Orton continued, "I assure you that I have not any place in your Scandinavian mythology."

Says Hamlet, somewhat puzzled: "Your words run glibly. But I do not understand what you are talking about."

Orton dismissed that not unexampled circumstance with a gesture of all-embracing benevolence; and he said furthermore:

"Nor have I offered to purchase your soul. I have drawn you into no entangling alliances, nor have I prompted you in any ill-doing. I have merely, out of my natural kindness, aided you to preserve your own life until you could fulfil your moral duty, as a loving son, by taking the life of King Fengon. With that obligation discharged, you have my free leave to enter Valhalla or whatsoever other paradise you may then find open. Ah, no, my dear Prince: my interest in the affairs of your family is philosophic. Your uncle Wiglerus paused to confer a few idle compliments upon Earl Sigmund's wife because she had a pleasingly tinted hide; and it entertains me to follow out the results."

"In fact, Wiglerus is now in Britain," Hamlet conceded, scratching his proud flaxen puzzled head. "But I do not see what my affairs have to do with the affairs of that strutting windbag."

"You will perceive the connection a great deal more clearly," Orton assured him, "by-and-by."

"But where and when?" says Hamlet.

"Ah, my Prince, before any long while—and as it so happens, here, upon this same beach of Straithkeld."

"Very well, then," said Hamlet, as he removed from his thumb the signet-ring of dead Horvendile. "I hail the omen. This place favors me. It is here that, at no cost whatever, I profit by your excellent advice. I infer that upon the beach of Straithkeld I shall meet with no adversary more hard to get the better of than is my vagabond uncle."

"And I—still, out of my natural kindness," returned Orton, caressing meditatively the small green crocodile on his cane,—"I assure you of that."

11

OF WIGLERUS IN THE WEST: EDRIC AND WIGLERUS TALK TOGETHER AT MID-DLEBURGH

WE MUST TAKE UP THE STORY AND CONCEDE THAT when the tidings reached Wiglerus of how his nephew had come into Britain, this news was greeted with a bland negligence. Wiglerus was in love; and beside that fact, neither Hamlet nor anything else seemed greatly to matter.

Truly, this was not the world-wandering Prince of Denmark's first love-affair, nor was it the last gallant trifling in which Wiglerus had figured since his polite vows of eternal fidelity when the extinction of Horvendile had forced Wiglerus to leave Thora Fairskin for the sake of his sister's shaken credit at Elsinore. He had thus lost Thora without losing any of that good taste which made him admire Thora; which still kept him a virtuoso of women; and which had enabled him to find, since the pleasing days of her brief and innocent reign, a fair number of faces well worthy of being admired, with the usual results. But the face of

Alftruda now seemed to him more dear than was any face which his memory held or which legend had made immortal. Never, the Prince assured himself, had it been granted to him, or to any noble poet in the times that were bygone, to behold in the course of a day, or during the dreams of a night, any creature so pure, or so sweet, or so beautiful; and he gave to Alftruda, then and there, his kindly time-battered heart.

So very casually, too (he reflected), had come about his meeting with Alftruda! It appeared to Wiglerus, nowadays, incredible that he had not always adored Alftruda. Yet in point of fact he had been upon a journey into Pictland, where a queen who at this time was no less famous for her beauty as a person than for her exploits as a warrior, and for her invincibility as a virgin, had been his goal. The existence of any such fair monster had seemed to Wiglerus, as a confirmed rambler among the world's quaint traps of chance and danger, a provocative; to the thinking of Wiglerus, this vainglorious woman required conquering more clamantly than did any dragon. So he had but paused overnight at Middleburgh for a glimpse of his former comrade in arms, King Edric, as Wiglerus rode northward toward the court of Queen Hermetrude; he had thus seen, in addition to Edric, Edric's daughter; and Wiglerus forthwith forgot all about this Hermetrude of Pictland, who would marry no man unless he first conquered her in battle. So far as went the new needs of Wiglerus, she was equally welcome to marry no intrepid vanquisher or to marry a ploughman or a ditch-digger or a devil, should she so elect, now that Wiglerus had need of no woman alive anywhere except the little Princess of Deira.

"I regret only," said Wiglerus, with a touch of appropriate emotion, to his life-long friend King Edric, "that for your daughter's sake I am not a better and younger Viking."

"You could well pass for both," replied the tall lean red-haired King of the Deiri. "Your conscience does not ever trouble you about anything; few saints can say as much: so what, pray, would you be gaining if you fell away into virtuous doings? Alftruda has enough virtue for two people, and in fact for two hundred, as you will be finding out in due course. She reminds me constantly of her dear mother, my poor Wiglerus. And for the rest, you glib small vagabond, you keep your youth to a marvel."

"That, Edric, is because I have with some care avoided the gross burdens of public esteem. You and Fengon, after a proper season of riot and misbehavior, were so imprudent as to settle down quietly into conformance with the better-thought-of platitudes. You have thus got your kingdoms and the good opinion of the world in general, at the price of your impaired hearing and your dimmed eyesight, of your failing teeth and of sundry wrinkles, under the caress of approving Time. But I—or such at least is my theory—I have kept on leading a life so unedifying that, as a well-thought-of deity, Time has preferred to avoid touching me."

"Your remarks, Wiglerus, retain their ancient custom of seeming, so near as I can follow them, to be nonsense."

"I trust so, Edric; for it does not become a young man who is heels over head in love to talk good sense."

"Then be off to your wooing, you scamp," says Edric.

"I obey you, my revered father-in-law," says Wiglerus.

12

OF ALFTRUDA: HOW SHE LOOKED AT TWO YOUNG MEN

So DID IT FOLLOW THAT WIGLERUS TALKED WITH Alftruda upon the wall of King Edric's fort. A curtain-wall topped with small parapets shaded them, quite comfortably, where they sat facing the river. Under the brisk western wind a mile or so of water dimpled and tossed, with a silvery glinting, in the sunlight of late afternoon; and upon the otherwise vacant river some two-score white-and-black ducks bobbed up and down rather inanely. Although their bodies were marked with varied patterns, each one of these ducks had a black head exactly alike, Wiglerus noted; each head faced northward; and the absurd creatures were not moving a feather. They apparently were not feeding; they submitted themselves to the immeasurable waters' motion, that was all; and they seemed well content to go on thus curtseying northward forever. They were like well-thought-of, stay-at-home persons who remembered always to dress and to behave as, for no special reason, did all other well-

thought-of persons, Wiglerus decided; and it made
you drowsy to look at them.

So he looked instead at Alftruda. He approved
of Alftruda. He honored her with the placid applause of a virtuoso. The child to-day was clothed
most becomingly, in this pale blue kirtle with a
plain silver belt; her glittering light hair, which
she wore loose after the custom of unmarried
women, reached down to her waist on both sides;
and it was tucked under her belt with praiseworthy
neatness.

Her eyes, he remarked—in the dependable
phrasing which, during the time of his verse-mak-
ing, he had found to be most efficacious when addressing blonde women,—were as bright and as
clear as dew on the grass of a May morning; her
skin was more white than the snow of a mountain
top or the swan on the wave; but her hair (as a
suitable tribute to erudition) was that Golden
Fleece hunted indomitably, in defiance of five in-
terjecting seas and between death's teeth, by the
fifty Argonauts, with entirely comprehensible zeal;
whereas her red young lips Wiglerus pronounced
to be just three times more sweet than honey which
is mixed through with red wine. In brief, Alftruda
was a wholesome, healthy and not very intelligent
young woman, with a fair share of good looks; but
Wiglerus happened to be in love with her.

His heart glowed with delight in her adorable primness; and she regarded him with tranquil affection.

It followed that, if upon this calm afternoon the ducks basking in the river were content, so likewise were the betrothed human couple above them upon the wall of the fort. Wiglerus was in love; and Alftruda was well pleased by the ingratiating prospect of marrying an accomplished and much talked about prince, whom she liked so sincerely just as he was that the notion of reforming him into a wholly different person appeared irresistible.

"—Though it is not really possible to think about you as a married man," she told him.

"Marriage will be the death of me," he agreed, —"inasmuch as it must end forever that which I have symbolized to my generation. Everywhere between Cathay and Lyonesse, and from Norway to the Nile, the passing of Wiglerus has ruffled the peace of nations; to-morrow Wiglerus will have become just another sedate and over-indulgent husband among the many millions of his confrères in indistinction. It ought to be a great trouble to your conscience, Alftruda, to know you have put out of living one of the most famous figures in folk-lore."

She asked his meaning; and he told her, at

once, with the complacent relish that an idealist always gets out of discussing himself.

"I refer, my dear, to a rather younger Wiglerus. Even until yesterday he remained, without any cowardly concessions to the changes of our latter-day degenerate time, that third prince who wanders at gay adventure among the implausible but soul-gratifying doings of a soundly built fairy tale. Every morning, Alftruda, that deceased rapscallion whom you have seen fit to inter, with the trowel of infatuation, in the bleak cemetery of desuetude, commended himself to fortune with a high heart; he gave a loose rein to the dandelion-colored steed, of that special breed which he preferred; and he let the stallion carry him where it chose, intrepidly, smilingly, and inquisitively. He thus roamed the world in quest of diverting adventures, which he did not fail to find. When there was need of fighting, he did not hold back from sword-strokes nor from murder at random: yet he always preferred—to do the young knave justice—to exhibit in cushioned places the humanizing and refining effects of rhetoric; and to profit by the contagious influence of a respectful devotion to womankind."

"Beyond any doubt," says Alftruda, "you think of this younger Wiglerus without disapproval."

"For that reason would you label me conceited? Alas, Alftruda, but I speak of a dead person. He is quite dead, that younger Wiglerus, whose portrait I have sketched for you as a slight memorial tribute."

"Even so," declared Alftruda, "we should not fail to look at the reverse of this picture. And I fear, dear lord, we would thus find it"—her lashes drooped, and her color heightened—"to be stained by the tears of misled womanhood."

The modest English maiden had conveyed her suspicions as to her lover's varied past with an admired correctness. Wiglerus, as a virtuoso, approved. And yet, along with the full tide of the admiration of Wiglerus the lover, was mingled a tributary stream of uneasiness. The quiet dignity of this calm cool child bespoke a sense of decorum which would always uplift—and it might be, even to uncomfortable altitudes—the blissful married life of Alftruda's husband. Well! but for her dear sake he was willing to become well-thought-of; he would conform, like those bobbing black-headed ducks down yonder, to whatever, for no special reason, seemed to be considered normal; and so, with a shrugging gesture, Wiglerus continued:

"You must not think that I present to you my portrait of the artist framed in a false gilding of lax moral principles. To the contrary! I remark

[68]

with stern disapproval that the coming of this fascinating and brilliant young stranger into the midst of a happy home circle did, now and then, alas, lead to results which involved the domestic peace of that household. Nevertheless, Alftruda, women could not but feel a very excusable interest in having their names made so famous as this gallant fine young poet, once, had it in his power to make any person; in order to purchase the glory of being praised in public by Wiglerus for one's beauty and virtue, a momentary surrender to him in private of these lauded possessions did not appear an excessive price; and so, since the gay rip was but human after all, a little injudicious behavior could not well but become the attendant of his chivalry—just now and then, Alftruda, and hardly ever in the day time. We should try to comprehend, rather than to abuse, the dear lad now he is dead."

Alftruda returned, with an indulgent sereneness: "We should try, instead, to find in the death of this shiftless wanderer the birth of a respected citizen. You have evaded the responsibilities of life, even from the first, with a levity which no truly affectionate woman could ever applaud. So we must try to change all that: for it is high time, my dear friend, you were sailing in command of your own fleet, and acquiring, from the heathen nations who do not worship Odin, your riches and plunder and renown, in the manner of a well-thought-of Viking gentleman."

"Yes," Wiglerus admitted with contrition; "now that I marry and settle down, it is my moral duty to become a ruthless and industrious pirate, like my peers. Yet, through some defect in my nature, I do not enjoy carnage; and though I have killed a fair number of adversaries, yet time and again I have got no great pleasure out of throat-cutting. It has seemed to me the act of a humorless person, to destroy any creatures so droll as I have found most human beings. You see, Alftruda, I lack your high standards of virtue; and so, I rather like human beings. Because of my deficiency in moral earnestness, I exterminate human beings with less pleasure than—I admit frankly—I derive from begetting them. To warfare I have preferred love. And yet"—his voice changed—"now that at long last I have found you, Alftruda, I perceive love may become somewhat frightening."

"How, if you truly care for me, Wiglerus," she inquired gravely, "can it seem to you terrible that I am to become your wife?"

"I have wanted only fine gay playfellows," he explained. "Now I myself have become the plaything of a force so strong that it troubles me. So I smirk, I fidget, and I talk a vast deal of nonsense, because at bottom I am terrified."

On a sudden the gallant Prince took her hand, kissing it, and he then touched her open palm with his fore-finger.

"All my happiness, all my future, lies here, at the disposal of a pure-minded, prudish, smug, ignorant, and very lovely child. That is an appalling thought. I would prefer to continue, as I have done always until to-day, my own carefree control of these matters."

"But if the hand be yours, you absurd Wiglerus, then all its contents are yours too, to dispose of as you elect; and besides that, I really do like you very much, sometimes, at least a little, I think."

He declared, with a grave and rather tender smiling:

"I am not worthy, my dear, of your regard, even when it is thus extensively qualified. Yet I shall try to become somewhat less unworthy, now I have said farewell forever to that good-for-nothing vagabond third prince; and so my saga ends upon an edifying note, and quite happily after all, does it not?"

Alftruda answered him: "But who can this be? I do not mean the two old ones."

She was standing at the high parapet, peeping over it, toward three armored horsemen who approached the fort. They came at a leisurely pace, across a level field, among dark twisted cedar-trees.

These trees seemed paralyzed and bent landward in a writhing effort to escape from the river's banks, Wiglerus observed idly. He observed also the small hands of Alftruda, the hands in which he had just placed his destiny, for now both of these hands touched the curtain-wall she was looking over. Their finger-tips were made quite white, he noted, by the intensity of her grip on the gray rough stone; and that unimportant detail, of her whitened finger-tips, stayed in the mind of Wiglerus for a long time.

"The young man in the middle," says Wiglerus, "is my nephew Hamlet. And the two gentlemen who accompany him are younger than I am."

"He is handsome," said Alftruda.

"Why, but indeed, my dear, with the sunset falling thus upon his gold-winged helmet, that stalwart tall young fellow, in his shining armor, has very much the appearance of a third prince come vaingloriously out of his fairy tale into this workaday Britain," replied Wiglerus. "So let us two go down at once to meet my insane but fine-looking kinsman at the south gate. It becomes chilly here. Or perhaps I have been depressed by the sad spectacle of his age-stricken infirm companions."

She said only, "You absurd Wiglerus!"

Yet the girl was now looking at him in a puzzled manner, he observed, and almost as if she were seeing for the first time her betrothed husband. So was it that they went away in silence from that quiet high place, and back into the onflow of their human affairs. They left behind them the unconcerned ducks, to bob up and down unnoted, where these birds continued to submit themselves, with an unhuman phlegm, to the immeasurable waters' motion.

13

HAMLET DOES NOT MAKE ANY FRIENDS IN DEIRA

WE MUST TELL OF HOW PRINCE HAMLET CAME TO Edric's castle, in company with the Earls Haakon and Olaf; and of how these last-named gentlemen brought with them, and duly delivered, the forged letter which in Fengon's name requested King Edric to see to it that Haakon and Olaf were hanged at once. Edric did not comply. He thought it more hospitable, and in far better accord with the nature of a large-hearted English gentleman, to allow both earls to attend the banquet which he had arranged in their honor; and so, upon the following morning, after they had both breakfasted undisturbed, their execution was attended to, in a pleasant field just windward of the castle's pig pens.

It seemed a thought awkward, however, that Fengon should be asking Edric to give his daughter to Hamlet in marriage, because in reply to this part of the letter the King of Deira could but explain to Prince Hamlet, with a polite feint of sympathy, that the King's only daughter was disposed of.

"Indeed, Wiglerus, it is excellent luck," said Edric, in private, "that Alftruda is safely promised to you. For if I dislike having to refuse Fengon's request, yet I would dislike still more to have my daughter married to a lunatic."

"I am less certain," replied Wiglerus, "of my very large nephew's insanity than I am of the fact that Alftruda looks at him rather more often than I, as his uncle by birth, would demand of her as his aunt by marriage."

Edric snorted.

"Who but an insane person would have behaved as did this Hamlet at the banquet I gave in honor of these troublesome Jutlanders? Nephew or no nephew, I must tell you frankly that if the gawky rude oaf had not been Fengon's son—"

The shapely and well-tended hand of Wiglerus was raised in protest.

"Dear friend," says he, "as a fairly competent Greek scholar, I cannot let pass your protasis. It reflects, you must let me remind you, upon the self-control of my sister when, if ever, she gave way to immoral impulses. I prefer to assume her never failing adherence to strait-laced conduct and all proper physical precautions. In the eyes of the law, and in his own eyes, Hamlet is the son of Horvendile."

"Yet, Wiglerus, you and I have some reason to know better."

"We have every possible reason, my dear Edric, to know better—as well-bred persons—than to admit any truth which is inconvenient."

"Yet it is equally inconvenient, Wiglerus, for a self-respecting king to have to put up with moonstruck insolence in his own banquet hall. The boy would eat or drink nothing; he scowled at everybody; and he chattered like a big tow-headed ape."

Wiglerus inclined to be more precise, as well as more charitable.

"He said, Edric, that he would not eat bread seasoned with a man's blood, or defile his throat with the rust of iron, or feed upon pork which tasted of raw human flesh: and I admit that to me a desire to do none of these things appears rational."

"He said also, Wiglerus, that he gave no respect to a misbegotten usurper. He remarked, casually, at my own table, that the late King of Deira was not my father."

"In fact, Edric, he did charge you, if but casually, with being a bastard. Well, and you have returned the compliment with unrestrained indignation. Honors are easy. So if I were indeed so fortunate as to be you, my dear friend, I would not pry into the truth or the untruth of Hamlet's post-prandial indiscretions. Let us ascribe the matter to your superb ale; and dismiss all to oblivion, escorted by a worldly-wise light shrug."

"Why, in Thor's holy name"—Edric grumbled—"should I submit to any such insults?"

"Because," replied Wiglerus, "since Truth is a goddess whom the discreet honor at a respectful distance, it is good policy to avoid grappling with a soothsayer. I dislike this affair, Edric. I would let it drop. I must tell you that I have made inquiries as to young Hamlet's indiscreet talking at your banquet."

"What of that?" says Edric.

The Prince of Denmark emptied his bronze goblet before replying. He paused also to stroke his chin, somewhat as if he suspected his beard of undue increase since he had last looked at it.

"Your swineherds," Wiglerus then answered, "tell me that only this summer your hogs found the body of a hanged thief and ate of its flesh."

"No doubt," said Edric; "for we hang in the next field. We have always hanged people there, Wiglerus; and I intend to continue the practice honorably. If the hogs get loose, then of course they behave like hogs. That is no reason why I should not behave like a gentleman, and go on keeping up our fine old English customs."

"Your corn," says Wiglerus, "was raised in a field where the armies of Anglia and Wessex fought once, a good century ago."

"Hah!" Edric replied, "but there are not many fields in any highly cultured country like Britain which the advance of civilization has not made fertile with blood."

"I applaud the apothegm," said Wiglerus: "yet I add that five very old swords, along with fragments of Roman armor, have been discovered at the bottom of the castle well, in the same water from which your ale was brewed."

Thereupon Edric said nothing, for some little while, but instead he weighed this new outcome with reflectiveness.

"Hamlet is indeed a soothsayer," was Edric's decision. "It is not our custom to keep armor in our drinking water. It would be bad for both of them. So he practises magic! He has no doubt a familiar spirit. Now, that sort of thing may be well enough on the Continent, Wiglerus, but here we do not hold with it. We consider it un-English. At any rate, the making of my ale and my bacon and my bread have not anything to do with my own making. They do not at all affect my begetting. That is the one important part of this affair; and I intend to get the real truth about my being in this disagreeable position—and in fact, about my being anywhere—from my mother."

Wiglerus sought counsel again at the bottom of his goblet; but he appeared to find there, instead, doubt flavored with religious scruples.

"Would it be kindly to distress Dame Gudrun, now that she has been a Druidess and has lived in pious retirement for so long, with such light talk about worldly matters?" Wiglerus debated, as if with himself. "Would it be advisable to set free the buzz of rumor and the wild tongue of gossip in the sedate dusk of her holy oak-grove?"

"I think—" said Edric.

"No: that is just what you fail to do," said Wiglerus; "since an actually thoughtful person would bear it in mind this vile slander is either true or not true. We both know it, of course, to be out of all reason; and for that same reason, with what anguish would the revered gentlewoman hear that an absurdity so atrocious is the reward of her long years of virtuous living!"

"But—" Edric said.

Wiglerus went on speaking, in the same instant that he extended his goblet for refilling.

"—Or let us boldly suppose the impossible," Wiglerus urged. "Let us imagine the charge to be well founded. Can we imagine that, on this account, the reviving of a remote peccadillo, committed per-

haps with that same girlish thoughtlessness which
you and I, as you must permit me to remind you,
Edric, have very often encouraged in young women
—would it, I repeat, be pleasant to Madam Gudrun? Would she think it filial? I can but appeal to
your better instincts."

"Still," said Edric, rumpling up his red hair
in desperation, "still, you spruce dried-up magpie,
why do you not let me speak one word to you, not
even edgeways?"

"Because you are far too garrulous," replied
Wiglerus; "and because you babble; and because
you babble injudiciously,—and keep re-hashing a
matter which, now you mention it, I have been at
some pains to investigate, and have found to be as
simple as are your notions about tact. I do not
know of any more scathing synonym for simplic-
ity."

Edric looked at him, very hard. And Wiglerus
beamed back in reassurance.

"Your good mother," Wiglerus said, "was
most happily blessed with a strong sense of duty.
Hah, and what then? why, after marriage her plain
duty, and in fact her paramount duty, was to provide the King of Deira with an heir."

"Yes," says Edric—confirming the mere truism somewhat forlornly.

"—And finding, after a long series of disap-

pointments, that as a collaborator his late Majesty
was, let us say—"

"I think, Wiglerus, we had better not say it."

"I agree with you, Edric. So I say only, without hemming or hawing, that the second groom of
the royal stables, as Dame Gudrun told me but
yesterday, was at that time a fine tall red-haired
young man; and that as the months prior to your
birth went by, what with one thing and another—
and through, no doubt, just a tiny touch of that
nervous irritability which the considerate person
will always condone in ladies who are in what we
term an interesting condition, and which nobody,
of course, would ever dream of condemning, or
even of taking quite seriously—why, that on account of these reasons, and perhaps yet other reasons, some little while before you were born, your
revered mother did think it expedient, and much
better in the long run for the higher interests of
everybody, to get rid of this red-haired groom."

"Hah!" said Edric.

"Yes," said Wiglerus. "He was hanged just
back of the pig pens. Well, and why not? As you
rightly observe, there is nothing like keeping up
these fine old English customs. And I agree with
you."

The ruddy, freckled and wholly uncompre-
hending face of red-haired Edric remained a minor

triumph of the art which conceals artfulness. That he lacked quickness of mind, nobody knew more clearly than did Edric; he had thus learned how useful it was to gain time for thought through a display of more obtuseness than he possessed; so he now said heavily:

"Good housewives have to be thrifty. That my mother should have decided to reduce expenses by getting rid of a groom does not seem to me worthy of any special comment."

"Nor to me; nor to any other person of any experience in the most commonplace of domestic conventions," replied Wiglerus. "Yet that is quite all there was to the quite normal sequence of events which my nephew—with the quite usual over-hasty judgment of youth—has quite misinterpreted."

Edric coughed. He swallowed his ale judicially. He said with decision:

"I rejoice to have the affair cleared up, and the stain of any possible scandal averted, by your never-failing tact, my dear friend. Let me entreat you to refill your goblet; for you have earned gallons. Nevertheless"—Edric added, between stiff lips—"I do not like this young Hamlet."

Wiglerus did not answer, in words. But he shrugged philosophically.

14

YET FURTHER RESULTS OF HAMLET'S SOOTHSAYING

AT THIS TIME ALL BRITAIN TALKED ABOUT THE soothsaying of Prince Hamlet at King Edric's banquet; and overnight, as it were, Hamlet had got a new name for deep knowledge and for his skill in dark arts. It was a famousness for which Hamlet paid nothing, as yet, and Edric not a great deal, because only two of the earls of Deira—his reputed cousins, Morcar and Ethelwulf—had refused to serve under the bastard of a stable groom; and they went into rebellion against him. That was troublesome for a while, but after one brisk week of ravaging and slaughter and high-minded oratory upon both sides, the fortune of war so far inclined to Edric that he got the pleasure of dealing handsomely with two persons for whom, despite his kindly nature, he still cherished the liking which is customary among cousins. For the first time in his life, Edric could regard Morcar and Ethelwulf with complete approval when their heads had been set up on iron spikes over the main gate of Middleburgh. He kept his throne thereafter with a strong hand; but he kept also an unloving opinion of Hamlet.

Nor did Hamlet's own uncle cherish the Prince of Jutland with an unadulterated affection. The boy had behaved without any tact, Wiglerus considered; it was quite unheard-of, that at any banquet the guest of honor should be laying bare the dietary shortcomings, and even the pre-natal past, of his host; and so through an excess of soothsaying (thought Wiglerus) Hamlet had failed in plain common civility. That was bad enough in itself; but far worse than this enormity had been Alftruda's too prompt forgiveness of it.

By not properly resenting any such orgy of ill-breeding Alftruda had made a display of misplaced virtue such as could not but upset an urbane admirer. For of what earthly use (Wiglerus debated) were nowadays the culture and the experience and the adroitness and the yet other shining merits which aforetime, in three quarters of the known world, had aroused masculine envy and put soundly to sleep the compunctions of female prudence? Wiglerus still possessed these courtly helpers, in full measure; yet as against Hamlet's mere animal youth and fine looks—thus Wiglerus had begun to suspect—they weighed as so many jack-

straws in the judgment of the young Princess of
Deira.

"My nephew," observed Wiglerus, "is pleasing
in face and form; he has not, I think, any more
brains than might be got with comfort into the
head of a house-fly, but one could not find a better
built male brute anywhere in the world. A peony
or the harvest moon is not more floridly colored.
He is, in brief, a superb oaf. So Alftruda gets great
pleasure in looking at him; her eyes travel constantly from spruce Wiglerus toward hulking
Hamlet; and daily, to those roving blue eyes, small
Wiglerus seems rather smaller, and a bit more in-
significant, and a vast deal older."

So was it that Wiglerus spoke with himself,
while his more forthright nephew spoke with Alftruda.

15

AN ATTACK AGAINST WIGLERUS
AGREED ON

SAID HAMLET, UPON THAT FINE SUNLIT MORNING: "Love has consigned me to a prison which none except love can open. I languish there, finding no mercy. When I see you I tremble with fear, like fire in the wind. I have no more reason left than a child possesses, so deeply am I troubled by my hunger for you. How can any kind-hearted person deny pity to a prince who is thus thoroughly upset?"

Alftruda's very pretty small face was now made yet prettier by her blushing to a suitable and proper extent. Alftruda replied calmly:

"I can refuse you neither pity nor love in my heart. But in action I must ask you to take your hand away."

"You are too prudish, Alftruda."

"No, my dear lord; but I am not married to you; and besides that, I am betrothed to somebody else."

"Yet if Wiglerus were to die, my love, you would not any longer be betrothed."

"That is logic," the Princess admitted, after giving to this deduction a moment of fair-minded consideration. "But I like poor Wiglerus."

"I," declared Hamlet, "do not like him. The old jackadandy is of a morbid and introspective type with which I have not any patience. I prefer action. For that reason I intend to kiss you."

He did so; and the Prince continued to speak, saying:

"I feel invigorated. I feel that Wiglerus must die. I feel that the sooner he does this, the better for our comfort. He has gone out alone to bathe. He is always bathing. He washes, all over, every day or so. Anybody would think the old fop was a fish. Let us likewise go out now. We will make a end of this inconvenient Wiglerus the instant his grinning face pops out of the water."

"That is a most shocking suggestion," Alftruda said, "because he will not have any clothes on, and it is not proper for an unmarried girl to be looking at naked men."

"You must get used to the naked male," replied Hamlet, fondly pinching her leg.

"Nor is it proper for you, my dear lord, to be killing an unarmed person."

"But why not?" said Hamlet, "since I intend

to pay a fair weregild for him. Besides that, his immoral conduct has disgusted my grandfather, King Rörek. Wiglerus makes free with women. He takes carnal liberties with women. When he was last in Elsinore he seduced a married lady, named Helga, whom King Rörek wanted for himself. The old gentleman became furious over such wickedness. Both the brothers of Wiglerus detest him. All will be more than glad to accept weregild in payment for his death. In that manner everything can be settled, honorably and inexpensively, without trouble."

Hamlet went down to the river bank, carrying an ax; and Alftruda followed him. So great was the tenderness of her heart that she protested, all the way, against the projected murder gently; and, with flushed embarrassment, she pointed out that, inasmuch as this special homicide would be viewed with disfavor by her father, he might, it was possible, become prejudiced against Hamlet as a son-in-law.

But the girl's sweet voice twittered up to, and about, her scowling lover without any effect. There was no dissuading the tall Prince of Jutland from his resolve to despatch Wiglerus first and these other troublesome matters afterward.

16

WIGLERUS GETS A BAD WOUND

When Hamlet, followed by Alftruda, got to the river bank, Wiglerus just then was coming out of the water, where his fine garments lay neatly arranged, in a bright blending of purple and white and gold, upon the green grass. So he said:

"Go away, Alftruda! And let me get some clothes on."

But Hamlet said, "Is it true, my uncle, that you have never run away from an adversary?"

Squatting back modestly into the water, Wiglerus answered:

"It is not in the least true, my nephew. An intelligent person will always run away when the odds against him are too heavy; but the point is that I wish Alftruda to run away. I in any event cannot run away without any clothes on."

"You are telling the truth," replied Hamlet, jovially, as he raised his ax. "You will be carried away from this river bank without any clothes on."

In the same moment, since under a descending ax-blade one has not leisure to nurture the proprie-

ties, naked Wiglerus leaped forward. Catching
Hamlet by the lower part of his legs, the older man
brought over the young blond giant, backward,
with a heavy fall. Wiglerus stooped to pick up the
ax, which his nephew had let drop. Hamlet,
a-sprawl on his back, cries out to Alftruda,—

"Are you going to stand there gaping while
this old spry devil kills me?"

"No, my dearest," said Alftruda loyally.

She caught up the short sword which Wiglerus
had been wearing, and with this she struck at Wiglerus, from behind, futilely but cutting open his
right shoulder. Wiglerus now had the ax. He con-
fronted his betrothed wife, naked and bleeding and
in a stir of frank surprise.

"So you would murder me, Alftruda!" He
gulped, just once. He said then:

"Get up, my nephew, out of that mud in
which, with an apt touch of symbolism, you are
now wallowing! And do you tell me the meaning of
this horseplay."

Arising, Hamlet remarked, "It means that we
love each other, old pot-belly, as no man and
woman have ever loved before."

"We intend," said Alftruda—with that sweet
firmness which she displayed always in repeating
any more familiar platitude—"to live our own
lives."

"And besides that," Hamlet blustered, "we despise the malice and the lewd envy of all skinny dotards."

Wiglerus answered: "O most absurd pair of assassins! I have sound reason to believe in the warmth of your shared affection. It has heated you, my nephew, into assaulting your near kinsman at a time when the infirm dotard was not merely unarmed but stark naked. And you, Alftruda, even your cool correctness, it has melted into an impulsive attempt to murder me, treacherously, with my own sword. Here is indeed a high flaming up of devotedness; here are love's ardors consuming the neat measures of every sort of good breeding into black cinders of infamy."

He spoke as with composure; yet there was never anyone, so his sick heart told him, at a worse disadvantage. He knew that he had been betrayed unpardonably and that his cause was righteous; he knew that behind him, in this moment of victory against large odds, thronged to support brave Wiglerus both honor and logic, abetted by a great galaxy of yet other major virtues: but he knew likewise that his heroism and his rightness did not at all matter. What mattered, to Wiglerus, was that both these young people hated him. What mattered was that young Hamlet and young Alftruda were looking, with a cruel delight, at his present lack of virility, and at his big drooping belly, and at his shapeless skinny legs, and at the other marks of advanced age which, in unsparing sunlight, his time-stricken, dripping wet, horrible nakedness showed to their arrogant youth.

Wiglerus said, to Alftruda: "Young people ought to be more considerate of their elders. You might have considered, for example, the circumstance that the heart in this vile casing is all yours. Your happiness is more dear to me than is my happiness. If you desire Hamlet to be your husband, then I also desire you should have Hamlet as your husband."

But he knew she was not thinking about his generosity of spirit, now that, like some incredible paladin of romance, he had flung down the battle-ax. He was sparing the forfeited life of Hamlet, and he was giving also to Hamlet the one woman whom heroic Wiglerus loved; but Alftruda was not weighing these superb actions in any at all proper attitude of tearful remorse. She was looking at the poor old man, instead, with simple and with slightly horrified interest. She was thinking, he felt, about how little hair this Wiglerus had on his gaunt body; and about how very ugly were the discolored broken veins on his thighs; and about how disgusting it would have been to have this impotent-looking, gross-bellied, lank ancient animal

as a bedfellow. Wiglerus suffered quite horribly under the cool inspection of his young lost love. In
fact, for that instant he rather disliked her.

Yet to Hamlet he said: "The happiness of Alftruda is more dear to me than is anything else in
this world. Do not forget that, my nephew."

Hamlet replied, nobly enough, "If ever my
faith fails her, my uncle, then let my head answer
for it."

"It shall," said Wiglerus in his anguish. "So
now, if only as a slight atonement to the ghost of
murdered decency, do the pair of you have the
kindness to go away; and let me put on some
clothes! I will arrange matters with Edric."

17

WHY WIGLERUS WENT NORTH, AND IN WHAT CONDITION

"I will arrange matters with Edric," Wiglerus had said, even in the moment of the ageing
adventurer's most bitter humiliation. About how
prodigally he made good his word, and about the
noble eloquence with which he made certain his
own unhappiness, the story speaks. The story tells
also about how King Edric, in part because of his
great love for his foster-brother Fengon, and in
part because of the wise arguments of Wiglerus,
agreed that Alftruda should marry Hamlet when
the last-named had come back from his faring into
Jutland.

—For in Jutland (so the Prince said) he had
debts as yet unpaid; he preferred to settle these
debts before he married; and besides that, it was,
of course, his proper duty to report to King Fengon that the Earls Haakon and Olaf had been
hanged properly. So for that while, Hamlet left
Deira.

Now it must be told how Edric talked yet further with Wiglerus.

"Dear friend," said Edric, "inasmuch as you have chosen to withdraw your pretensions, and since my daughter is so obtuse as not to have observed this Hamlet is, by long odds, the most objectionable ruffian whom an unexplained oversight on the part of Providence as yet allows to continue living anywhere, outside a prison, I have given to Hamlet a parent's fond blessing. It is possible you may infer, from what I have said, that I do not love your nephew. I agree with your inference. I concede that, as our proverb has it, the guess of the wise man is truth. Hamlet possesses no tact. Hamlet has put me to the expense of a civil war through his incivility in disputing, at my own dining table, the rectitude of my birth. Hamlet has dipped Britain into a gurgling hell-broth of demented gossip about my hither-to respected mother, Dame Gudrun, and some red-haired stable groom or another. People everywhere, I can assure you, are talking about this ancient, quite probably untrue, and wholly irrelevant matter. I feel that horses look at me in a manner far too familiar; I am certain the lower classes of Deira neigh and whinny whenever I appear in public; and yet by the dictates of policy I am forced not to resent these unpleasing phenomena. In a situation made thus awkward, I cannot find its contriver congenial. Still, just as you have pointed out, Hamlet is heir to Jutland; and in this capacity he might, I admit, be regarded, by merely mercenary idiots, as a desirable match. Moreover, this infernal Hamlet is the son of my own foster-brother Fengon—"

Wiglerus said: "But come now, Edric! even in our joint anguish, let us remain well-bred. As before to-day I have had the honor to point out, my nephew is the son of my sister. He must, in all polite logic, at his age, be the son of her first husband rather than of her second husband."

"He shall have any father you prefer," returned Edric generously. "Yet even though you supply him with a dozen fathers, my dear Wiglerus, they cannot poultice my regret over not having you here at Middleburgh to talk nonsense forever."

"But we do not part for long, let us hope," says Wiglerus. "It is only that I have resumed my old fancy of going northward into Pictland on account of what I have heard about Queen Hermetrude."

Edric disapproved.

"You would do far better to avoid that fine vixen. She is a bad lot. She despises marriage, because she does not esteem any man worthy to be her husband. She has killed—at times with the aid of her dark headsman Magnus, and at yet other times with her own strong handsome hands, so they tell me,—every man who desired her to marry."

"Do you be of good cheer, Edric, for whatever else I may ask of Dame Hermetrude, I shall not ask marriage," Wiglerus answered; and he so went northward.

He went most handsomely, in a gilt saddle, riding as was his custom upon a tall dandelion-colored stallion, of the rare breed imported out of Iceland; and he wore a fine scarlet cloak lined with fox fur and trimmed with gold bands. The trappings of his horse likewise were of scarlet. Wiglerus was, in brief, a resplendent figure, even from the fluted wings of his gilt helmet to the twinkling rowels of his gilt spurs; but his cheeriness stayed external.

For Wiglerus nowadays (so he told himself) was the heart-broken victim of a never-dying unhappiness. The fact that he had lost Alftruda forever seemed beyond rhetoric, for despite every canon of good taste, he found himself to be still in love with a young woman who had done her feeble utmost to murder him. Nor was that, by any means, all. In addition to his person, Alftruda had attacked his pride, by preferring Hamlet; and moreover, through this unaccountable choice, had revealed her complete lack of good judgment. For any young woman not to succumb to Wiglerus, one admitted, might be passed over, just in itself, as a not unexampled aberration, inasmuch as Wiglerus could remember no less than four other eccentric ladies who at odd times had held out against his love-making. But when it came to giving up a rather notably well-bred person in favor of a gross lout, who discouraged bathing with a battle-ax—why, but Alftruda had simply flaunted to the polite world at large the inferiority of her taste! All virtuosi would now criticize Alftruda most unfavorably.

Wiglerus could not attempt to deny the rustic openness of her gaucherie; nor to the other side, could he deny that he still loved Alftruda; and for this reason he now went, on his journey away from her, without any companions except only his grief and his inveterate gallantness. It is possible (the tale says here) that both of these would have been less strong had he foreknown how the mishaps behind him compared with those he approached.

18

SIWARD SWIFT-FOOT COMES INTO THE STORY

Now it was in this same journey, they relate, that Wiglerus had trouble with Aslaug of Grange over a cloak made out of ostrich feathers; the story tells about the strange end of this quarrel: and they say also that, two days later, in some woods near Trunborough, Prince Wiglerus fought against Siward Swift-Foot.

Siward was disapproved of in these parts because of the indiscrimination with which he robbed and killed the people whom he waylaid. But Wiglerus he did not rob, or kill either, even though, at about the middle of the second stanza of a love-song which the Prince of Denmark was gloomily emitting, the outlaw attacked this vagabond chorister with such suddenness and ferocity that Wiglerus was hard pressed; and at first gave way.

Then it was Wiglerus who got the better in this affair, for the world-wandering Prince had fought many good fights and understood the right use of arms as well as did any famous captain or other sort of hired murderer then living. Through a trick which Wiglerus had mastered in the green rice-fields of Pavia, he toppled his opponent from the saddle in the same instant that he wrested the sword out of Siward's hand; and Wiglerus sat astraddle upon Siward's chest, holding a dagger at the forest-man's throat.

The thief laughed upward, defiantly. His large bear-skin cap had tumbled from his head. You thus saw that Siward Swift-Foot had a fierce, thin and very proud face. The mocking handsomeness of this face was strange—and yet somehow it appeared familiar—in its dark framing of the outlaw's long hair, which spread out upon the ground, untidily, among small knotty pine-twigs and pale brown pine-needles.

"You fight well," says Siward, quite at his ease. "But I do not fear you, old Cut-and-Twist, not even in these straits. It was foretold of me that I should not die in any human battling, but only at the desire of my divine father; for I come of an immortal race."

"That is interesting," declared Wiglerus.

"It is far more than interesting," said the forest-man, "inasmuch as it is true."

"You have wounded me in two places," said Wiglerus, "and each place hurts. I incline, for that reason, to test the truth of your immortality with this knife point. Who are you?"

"I am Siward Swift-Foot."

Wiglerus said: "At Turnborough I was told as much; and I was told also that in these woods you deny the loving guidance of Odin the All-Father, with a rather untactful candor; you worship a heathen god; you rob travellers; and you kill such of them as will not bow down to your god. All this I know about you, Siward Swift-Foot. But I do not know from whom you stole that ruby ring on your finger."

The thief cried out, "I did not steal it from anyone, for my ring was fetched to me from heaven nine months before I was born."

"Your story assumes an increasing interest, Siward Swift-Foot, at—if you will permit the observation—the cost of some likelihood."

"But my mother was tall beautiful dark Athlinn of Marna," the thief said, "and it was with this ring that a young god married her and begot me to be his son."

"Oh! ah! but now I follow you," said Wiglerus: "and yet I imagine that you do not know the name of this god, because no doubt he came and he went incognito, as is customary in such immortal amours."

"He did nothing of the sort," replied the forest-man; "for my divine father is called Wiglerus."

"Why, but to be sure; for I have heard of him before to-day," said Wiglerus, "but not of his deification."

"And at his own good hour, you grinning old rascal, divine Wiglerus will return, in the bright glory of his never-fading youth, and then he will restore the youth of my mother, and he will receive us both into his heavenly kingdom."

"You tell me nothing unnormal," replied Wiglerus; "for these high reunions of the family circle are the usual promissory notes of gods who beget children upon mortal women. So it was the mere truth they reported, at the village tavern, that you have a shrine in these woods where you compel people to worship your begetter, this so wonderful Wiglerus; and where your aged mother, even to-day, serves as his priestess. This world is a droll place, Siward Swift-Foot! Still, even among so many outbursts of insane humor, it is a proud lot to be the child of a god and the inheritor of a kingdom in heaven. I wish you much joy of it."

Wiglerus sighed then. He sheathed his dagger. He rose up from sitting upon his own flesh and blood.

"Now, stout old fighter," Siward cried out, "now you shall go with me to worship my father in his immortal youth."

Wiglerus said: "No; for his youth was not immortal. His youth has gone out of this Wiglerus, and he no longer is all wonderful. He is only a strutting fribble, a little puzzled and a little frightened, at the dark bottom of his withered cold heart, because the great glory of our human life is youth; and his youth is bygone."

"We must fight again," said Siward, catching up his long sword from out of a fern clump, "for I will not listen to any such blasphemies against Wiglerus."

"Be still, dear fool," said Wiglerus.

"Indeed I shall not be still, you old wicked unbeliever; for I intend to rip the red heart out of you and leave it here to be the food of the gray wolf and the black crows."

"I regret," said Wiglerus, "to deny your strong sense of filial gratitude its customary exercises. Yet I highly value my heart; not only am I attached to it by force of habit, but its indiscretions, off and on, have afforded me a vast deal of entertainment: and so I shall not leave my heart in this place."

"You leave your life in this place," cried Siward.

Then he rushed forward, with his long sword aloft, and he struck furiously at the unguarded head of Wiglerus, in the same instant that Wiglerus stepped sideways, avoiding the blow. Wiglerus thrust his sword, with both hands, into Siward's middle, so that it pierced the young outlaw's belly from the left side even to the right side.

Siward grunted. Afterward Siward Swift-Foot cried out, with a great voice,—

"It is ended."

He tumbled forward, shivering. He moaned like a hurt dog. He twitched his very broad shoulders, just twice, as he lay face downward among the brown pine-needles. His black tousled head touched a small vine, of which the rather dark green leaves were divided each into five petals, Wiglerus noted. Or was it "petals,"—the correct name for the sub-divisions of a leaf? One must find out. One had, meanwhile, one's paternal duties.

Wiglerus turned over the body. Then Siward smiled up at him, with an odd blending of joy and of agony, of wonder and of proud faith. He said, gasping,—

"Into your hands—my father,—I commend my spirit."

He died at that instant.

"I regret this mortal outcome;" said Wiglerus, looking considerately into the tortured young face. "But I could not avoid the excesses of my son's piety. And I am not horror-stricken, so far as I can perceive, now that I end the existence of a matured germ which once spurted out of me. It seems very much like killing any other human being. I have

never enjoyed killing anybody except Gissur Syr—
and perhaps Vagn, when I was too young to know
better—and then, of course, there was Faidit of the
Rocks, down in Portugal."

Yet Wiglerus rode onward thinking rather
wistfully as to remote happenings. Very truly he
had been a dashing rapscallion then, in the full
strength of his young manhood; and Athlinn, even
though she was older than he, proved a fit mate
for him, during that one night they had spent together. It had been extremely tactful of her, to
pass off the results as the fruitage of a divine visita-
tion; women had excellent taste, which at all seasons
flowered superbly under the heat of social dilemmas.
Athlinn had converted what might have been a
family scandal into a signal honor to her family—
even though, after so many years, no doubt, poor
shrivelled doting Athlinn had come quite to believe
in her own taradiddles. Women usually did end by
believing what they preferred to believe.

You had always remembered the ring,—
though, at this distance in time, you could not
quite recollect whether it were Yolande or Beatrix
who gave to you this ring—for it was a girl in
Provence, you were almost certain—as a pledge of
eternal fidelity. You remembered also, with smiling
tenderness, that heroic gesture with which you had
placed this ring upon Athlinn's finger, bidding her

keep it until her child's thumb should fit it. The ruby which was inset in this ring you had compared to your own bleeding heart, rather effectively. All your trafficking with that splendid, full-bosomed, dark-haired, pleasantly plump woman had been conducted in the very best vein of romance, even up to the moment of your final parting, at red dawn, in a noble and most satisfactory seizure of despair.

So it could not but be an anti-climax, and a sad floundering into the bathetic, for you to find this ring upon the too-acquisitive hand of an inurbane ignorant highway robber, who was your own grown-up son, well upon his way to the public gallows. From any such degrading elevation you —at worst—had now rescued Siward Swift-Foot; now, yet again, the ring adorned your own finger, where it belonged, as a pledge of eternal fidelity to whoever she was. That the young bad-smelling ruffian worshipped you, and even went to the extreme length of murdering people who did not worship you, seemed rather touching. Athlinn would grieve for his death—that Athlinn who to-day was a withered gray half-witted hag. The people of Turnborough would no doubt burn Athlinn as a witch, now she was defenceless. Happenings of this sort were depressing—even though, to be sure, there must be a great number of your former sweethearts and of your various children roving about, nowadays, in a world so perplexing and so treacherous that some few of them must necessarily come to distressing ends.

Such were the sedate reflections of Wiglerus, as he pensively rode northward to try the luck of an ageing and kindly and self-centered adventurer with the famous Queen Hermetrude of Pictland.

19

OF THE NEWS WHICH WAS BROUGHT
OUT OF JUTLAND

WE MUST GO BACK AND TELL ABOUT HOW A MES-
senger came to the King of Deira from the King
of Jutland; and about how, of this affable gray
person, it was demanded by tall red-haired Edric,—

"What news do you bring from our esteemed,
if, as we regret to admit, remote, but nevertheless
beloved, brother of Jutland?"

"My lord King, I bring first of all the news"—
was the reply—"that Prince Hamlet arrived safely
at the King's palace in Sundby yesterday morning."

Says Edric: "What is this lunacy? How can
you tell what happened in Jutland yesterday morning?"

"Why, Majesty, but I was there at the time.
Who, pray, can be better fitted to give you an account of your future son-in-law's home-coming
than anybody who was an eye-witness of it?"

"Your question has a superficial flavor of
logic," replied Edric, stroking his short beard, with

that special effect of lurking cunning which the dull-minded exude before the uncomprehended; "but only," the King added pouncingly, "so far as it goes." After having thus demolished, with a sound formula, all this gray knave's deceit, King Edric said,—

"We do not know your name."

"Nor do many other mortals, my lord King; but at present I am called Orton."

"Why, then, Orton, it seems to us that if you were in Jutland yesterday, and are in Britain to-day, you travel altogether too quickly, for a crippled person."

"Do you not think it suitable, Majesty, that a monarch so famous as is Edric, King of the Deiri, should be served without thought of one's physical infirmity and with all possible haste?"

"We do not deny that, you gray grinning Orton. It is only that nobody—except perhaps a fiend—could be serving us with any impossible haste."

Orton was grieved by this observation; and he said, with an air of pious reproof,—

"Beyond doubt, my lord King, you speak heresy, since a blessed spirit needs to be quite as nimble and just as apt to be attending to your comfort."

"My friend, you have not the look of a blessed spirit."

"Yet that, my lord King, is not altogether the point which it has pleased your most gracious Majesty to raise; and the question we are now weighing, so far as I can understand it, is whether or not I resemble a fiend?"

"How do we know?" returned King Edric conclusively. "What do you mean by insinuating that we are upon terms of intimate acquaintance with any fiends? We consider fiends, you must let us tell you, to be un-English. Why do you keep arguing about fiends? Does it matter to us whether you are a fiend or a blessed spirit, or a bachelor or an orphan, or a wild-rose bush, in your private life? Quite the contrary! It is in the capacity of a herald that you approach us. It is in the capacity of a herald that you have been received at our court and that you sit in our hall of audience grinning like a gray drunken skeleton over the handle of your cane. So now, in high Heaven's name, do you discharge your errand by speaking your message! and stop talking!"

"I hear; I tremble; I obey," replied Orton: "and in brief, I shall tell you what happened yesterday, in the banquet hall of the most lordly castle of the King of Jutland, just as Gervendile Cut-

Throat builded it out of pine-wood and maple-wood, in the fields east of Sundby."

I must first declare to your Majesty (Orton resumed) that inasmuch as Queen Geruth had despaired of her son's life after his prolonged absence, Prince Hamlet entered the banquet hall of King Fengon, by an unexampled chance, upon the forenoon of his own birthday, when the funerals of Prince Hamlet were being celebrated by the stout earls of Jutland. The surprise occasioned by his return I leave you to imagine; the joy was somewhat more temperate. The earls of King Fengon were not delighted to have back this Prince who carried under his arm a bundle of sharpened sticks, and whom they esteemed to be insane.

They had cause for this suspicion; for Prince Hamlet appeared to recall no one of them; he professed not ever to have heard of any persons called Haakon or Olaf; and proclaimed that he himself was not a prince but only a butler in search of employment.

"Do you humor this seeming madman," says King Fengon, moodily, "but nail fast his sword into its scabbard, lest he hurt somebody."

This was done. The King then withdrew, tak-

ing with him the five sons of Corambus, in order
that they might consult as to the best way of dis-
charging their joint obligations to honor and quickness of action.

But of the gentry who remained in the banquet hall, each high-born pirate busied himself to
adorn with intoxication these merry funerals, at
which the lamented person himself played the butler and attended on his mourners. All ate and bel-
lowed with unrestrained laughter, while they drank
again and yet again to the better health of the ob-
sequious corpse. Prince Hamlet did not for one instant suffer the pots or the goblets or the drinking-
horns to remain empty: he served all with the
impetuosity of a statesman who is spending the
money of the public. He in this way managed to
add to the ale and mead the drugs with which a
friendly familiar—whose name is not of immediate
consequence—had the honor to furnish him.

The noblemen of Jutland, being thus stuffed
with meat and stupefied with drugs, began by-and-
by to sleep in the same place where they had dined.
They one and all reposed snortingly upon the
rushes, like gorged hogs, when Prince Hamlet
ripped away the upper part of the new red-and-
gold tapestries which adorned the banquet hall,
leaving the bottom of these tapestries nailed fast to
the wall. He pulled down these tapestries over the

snoring earls of Jutland, like coverlets. He fastened each tapestry to the ground, very tightly, with his sharp wooden sticks. He locked up the doors of the hall, with bolts, from without. He set fire to the four corners of the building of pine-wood and maple-wood.

No victim escaped alive from that great burning. Instead, as the Prince remarked to me, in a pleasing vein of friendly humor, they were all forced to purge their sins with fire, and to dry up the wicked abundance of liquor in their pampered bodies, by the inevitable and hungry flames of that bonfire with which Hamlet of Jutland commemorated his birthday.

"Such murderings of the defenceless," declared King Edric, "were the acts of an insane brute. Only, there is not any cur, or snake, or hyena, so naked of decency; the very crocodile, there on your cane, would turn from green to red with embarrassment if he were charged with such wicked doings."

"Your pardon, Majesty," replied Orton, "but we face here the acts of a far-seeing statesman. The earls of Jutland were intelligent persons; they had judgment; and so they were dangerous. These earls approved of King Fengon, because he ruled over his province with thrift, and with foresight, and with rationality. It thus became needful to dispose of these old-fashioned and illiberal-minded people. I will now discourse yet further concerning the high deeds of Prince Hamlet."

King Fengon, as I have told you (Orton resumed), had withdrawn very early from this disorderly feasting, which did not agree with a monarch of his quiet and temperate habits and infirm digestion. He had arranged everything with the sons of Corambus. The peace-loving King had managed to divert them from picking any public quarrel with Hamlet, by giving them the keys to the guest room in which Hamlet was to pass the night, so that they might obey the dictates of honor by killing the Prince in his sleep without disturbing the law and order of Jutland. With the King's duty thus well discharged, and after the sons of Corambus had gone back to the banquet hall—to be converted, alas, into charred bones, along with one hundred and thirty-nine other gallant sea-robbers, —King Fengon was indulging in the healthful afternoon nap recommended by his physicians.

Hamlet therefore entered the King's bedchamber unperceived. He took up Fengon's sword; and in place of it, he laid down his own sword, which by the King's orders had been nailed into its scabbard. Hamlet cried out, in an exultant voice,—

"I wonder, King of Jutland, to see you sleeping so quietly when you are thus near to ruin."

"What is here?" says Fengon, starting up from the bed.

"Here is the end," said Hamlet. "Here is the end of power, and of applause, and of comfort, and of secret murderings, and of incest."

"Is it so, my son?" Fengon answered, regarding the drawn sword; and with a blue coverlet half about him, he sat there on the side of his bed, blinking with dazed eyes as if the shining steel dazzled him.

Said Hamlet: "That same sword with which you killed Horvendile has turned against you. The son of Horvendile is at hand to avenge the death of his father."

Fengon wasted no words. He leaped quickly, but he stumbled as he clutched at the laid-by sword of Hamlet. While the King tried to pull it from the scabbard in which he had ordered it to be fastened, then Hamlet gave him such a blow upon the neck that the gray head of Fengon was cut half away from his body by Fengon's own sword. He died instantly, with his feet yet entangled in a blue coverlet.

Hamlet said: "This just and violent death is

your fit reward. Now go your ways, lost soul of Fengon. Do you tell the great soul of Horvendile that he is avenged honorably."

In this manner did Hamlet destroy single-handed the King of Jutland and all his court and the King's banquet hall to boot. In this pleasant vein of romantic irony, by killing his own father, did Hamlet avenge the death of his uncle.

"The death of Fengon likewise," returned Edric, "shall be avenged."

He spoke quietly.

"Beyond doubt, it is the duty of a foster-brother," said Orton, "to exact for this honorable assassination an honorable vengeance. Dear me!"— the gray man declared, with an approving and amicable chuckling,—"but this thing called honor is truly a fine virtue! I think it the most useful of all virtues in these north parts of the world; and there is nobody living who values honor more highly than I do."

Edric said only, "Where now is this parricide?"

"Why, but of course he is in the position for which his late self-induced bereavement qualified him," replied Orton, a shade surprised—"upon the throne of Jutland. Hamlet was Fengon's heir. The

upper classes of Jutland had been happily and almost completely disposed of. To the less intelligent
riffraff Prince Hamlet addressed himself, in search
of their mandate, through an oration which I had
the pleasure of drafting. It rather handsomely justi-
fied his attack upon the wicked forces of greed and
privilege and oppression,—or so, at least, I was told
by unbiassed observers. As the author of his remarks, I might not presume to judge their exact
worth; and besides, I have aided in the preparing of
far too many such orations to regard them with
seriousness. In brief, he bamboozled the improv-
ident gross-witted proletariat, after an ancient and
time-approved fashion, beside the yet smoking
ruins of the banquet hall, in what he described,
rather humorously, as a fireside chat. He promised
them a reduction in all government expenditures
at once; and a balancing of the budget next year
through the use of counterfeit money; and a more
abundant living for everybody, now that pensions
would replace taxes; and a renewal of indefinite
prosperity; and no more war, or disease, or bad
weather; and every other handsome sort of insanity
which happened to occur to me. They believed him
of course, very uproariously, because in all known
lands it is the quaint trait of popular sentiment to
dislike any sort of rationality and to find truth

unpatriotic. So all passed smoothly; and the accession of King Hamlet was received with delight by his loyal subjects."

"We comprehend," said Edric, who had now re-assumed a regal stateliness of demeanor. "We infer it is as the ambassador, not of poor Fengon, but of this eternally damned King Hamlet that you come to us."

"I come, Majesty, rather as his forerunner; and to announce that the new King of Jutland is forthwith sailing toward Britain to marry your daughter."

"Hah!" says Edric; and into this monosyllable he got a great deal more of annoyance than of hospitality.

"Nor is there, I imagine, any princess or a queen in all Britain," Orton continued, as he meditatively twirled about the handle of his orangewood cane, "who would not very gladly become his wife, now that Hamlet is a monarch in his own right, and does not have to consider anybody but his liege-lord, the King of Denmark."

"Hoh!" says Edric.

"Yes, Majesty: you correct me. One does have to except the Queen of Pictland," Orton admitted: "for, as I perceive you were going on to remind me, Dame Hermetrude abhors marriage so utterly that she fights with, and she puts to death, even the ambassadors of such kings as dare to propose marriage to her. That seems to me a pity: I am a great believer in marriage. Yet thus, no doubt, she would murder King Hamlet also if he dared to talk to her about marrying him, or even about marrying you, my lord King, as your seventh wife."

"You gray babbler," said Edric, in nettled surprise, "what have we to do with the Queen of Pictland? or with whether she marries or does not marry?"

"Nothing whatever, Majesty,"—was the bland answer,—"and I truly hope that you may not ever meddle with the ferocious woman by sending her any ambassador whom you desire to continue in living. But my thoughts wander," said Orton, with a bright smile of apology, "for I had meant only to tell you that the new King of Jutland is sailing at once toward Britain and the dear presence of your daughter."

"His coming will be welcome," returned Edric, "since otherwise we would think it needful to go to him, at the head of our army."

20

WHAT EDRIC HAD TO THINK ABOUT HONORABLY

IT IS TOLD HOW EDRIC ACTED WITH THE UNHASTY and dogged high-mindedness of a British gentleman brought nose to nose with a debt in honor and the possible advantages which he might get out of not ignoring, greasily, its undeniable existence. He remembered not merely that love which had been between Fengon and Edric. He remembered also how, at Volsoddi, in the days of their youth, he and Fengon with all proper solemnity had cut away from the ground three loops of turf, leaving both ends of each loop attached to the ground; and how they had passed together under these loops. Each boy had drawn blood from the other's hand. They had let their blood mingle in the earth under the digged-up turf. They were thus made foster-brothers.

Of all the moral obligations which existed among honest and refined Vikings, the obligations of a foster-brother were the most sacred and the most unbreakable. This, Edric reflected, was not like a war debt incurred at the light cost of pledging faith to a nation who knew no better than to take your word in a matter which concerned money; this was a personal debt; and so, Edric had not any choice, in honor, except to avenge the death of Fengon.

It was because of such stringent obligations, indeed (the tale says here), that, at Volsoddi, Wiglerus had declined to share in these holy ceremonies, although young Wiglerus, who even then was serving an apprenticeship in frivolity, had accounted for his holding-back upon other grounds.

"I am already endowed, it may be for my sins, with two brothers," said Wiglerus; "and the problem of deciding whether I dislike Thorfin or Einar the more heartily is enough for me. With four brothers, my mentality would be wrecked, among raging seas of abhorrence. No, my dear friends: I prefer to go on regarding both of you without the ugly and all-grudging fervor of fraternal affection. I have found brotherhood to be an affliction of Providence such as the philosopher does not augment."

Well, but to the other side (Edric continued his reflections), young Hamlet was now Edric's own son-in-law; and Alftruda stayed in love with the atrocious, self-complacent, tall parricide, who as yet accepted her devotion, without any

complaint, as a mere matter of course, condescend-
ingly. Alftruda would be quite unreasonable about
Hamlet's destruction. The intrusion, of her absurd
folly, into the affairs of honor of a properly reared
Englishman, was awkward; for if only the insane
girl had shown the good taste, and the plain common-sense, to prefer Wiglerus, instead of letting
him wander off into wild Pictland and into the
dubious company of that murderous Queen Hermetrude, then you would confront no difficulty at
all! It was a lament which gave Edric his cue, now
that he thought over the diffuse babblings of that
gray lame simpleton, Orton.

For a king (Edric remarked, to himself, with
a pleased look, such as upon an unregal face might
have been called simpering) it was a handy art, thus
to be able to unearth, even from out of such incon-
sequent gossip, a fact of importance. Edric could
not but admire his own cleverness; and by this
striking instance of it he was made genial, now
that he saw how to keep faith with his honor as an
Englishman without very much incommoding himself.

21

HAMLET WINS THE APPROVAL OF HIS FATHER-IN-LAW BY LOSING HIS TEMPER

WE MUST TELL ABOUT HOW THE AGEING KING OF the Deiri began to treat the young King of Jutland with fond affability, and to entreat Hamlet not to return homeward.

"—For I shall be very lonely," says Edric, "if ever my dear daughter—or you either, of course, my dear son-in-law,—were to leave me. My loneliness would be quite unendurable, now that I have no wife. I have been so unfortunate as to lose six wives, Hamlet, one after another, though I did not divorce but two of them; and never while any one of those noble orators was able to speak to me in private, here at Middleburgh, with candor, for my own good, did I know a single moment of loneliness, or of quiet either."

"Why then," asked Hamlet, "do you not tread a seventh wife, you red cock-sparrow?"

Edric gaped, in frank wonder.

"Upon my word, Hamlet, but you astound

me! for out of hand you have found a solution for my problem. You think very quickly, Hamlet."

"An adroit mind is merely a gift of nature," said pleased Hamlet with proper modestness. "So I deserve no special credit for having one."

"Still, son-in-law"—Edric continued, after a moment of reflection,—"still, I would have to marry suitably. I would have to marry a queen. And in all Britain, or at any rate in all Britain south of Pictland, there is no queen who stays unmarried."

"Yet in Pictland, sir, Queen Hermetrude has no husband."

"To think now," Edric remarked, in high admiration, "of my having overlooked Queen Hermetrude! My wits must be failing me. But you, Hamlet, overlook nothing; your suggestions become more and yet more excellent; and I envy you the trenchant clearness of an agile and never sleeping intelligence."

"Perhaps—you flannel-mouthed fine flatterer, —perhaps it was because you yourself mentioned Pictland," Hamlet hazarded in supreme good humor.

That might have led him, Hamlet continued, to think about just where to get for his gay old goat of a father-in-law a renewal of pleasures such as Hamlet now named. He particularized.

And Edric winced at the young blackguard's coarseness, which he did not find in harmony with the ways of an elder generation,—by whom the indecorous had been robbed of indecorum through robing it, in talk, with paraphrases, and during enactment, with silence. But Edric kept on smiling.

"Yes, Hamlet; it is just as you say. I myself mentioned Pictland; and to my mind that makes my obtuseness still more remarkable. Yet now I reflect upon your plan—and the really brilliant plan which you are proposing to carry out, my dear Hamlet,—why, I remember that this queen refuses to marry."

Hamlet, in reply, acknowledged that for a moment he had forgotten the coy notions of the young bitch; and granted the rumor that this Hermetrude had killed all men who talked to her about a natural function which Hamlet again mentioned.

Edric said hastily: "And that would be a drawback, Hamlet. You see, not any one of my earls would dare to act as my ambassador and ask her to marry me."

"King Edric, your earls are a poor lot. They are not sound workmen. They do not fetch with them the proper tools with which to manage these prim-talking women."

Hamlet then gave his own opinion, at some

length, as to the real needs of any woman who spoke about remaining a virgin forever; and, as a gentleman of the old school, Edric did not wince. He shuddered. Still, Edric kept on smiling.

"Ah, but, my dear boy," says he, "this Hermetrude is beyond any man's management. She is bold as Thor, as shrewd as Loki; the gods might control her, but hardly any mortal. I question if even the daring and subtlety of a Hamlet could get the better of her."

At this sort of nonsense, proud Hamlet frowned. He shattered it, with an heroic loftiness, by saying:

"Yet my daring and my subtlety got the better of Fengon. They got the better of his entire court. They got the better of all Jutland, not so very long ago."

"Yes; that affair was quite prudently managed," Edric granted in frank approval,—"without any least risk to you. There is nobody but must admire the cool judgment you displayed. Drugged men could not hurt an infant in diapers; nor could you very well, of course, continue to be afraid of Fengon after you had found him unarmed and asleep."

"I was not ever afraid of Fengon," said Hamlet curtly.

Edric was all apology, even from his red hair

to the gilt heels of his fine boots of cordovan leather.

"Ah, but, my dear boy, but I grant it freely that a not particularly bold person would have far more reason to be afraid of Queen Hermetrude."

"What the devil do you mean, King Edric?" said Hamlet, half rising up from his chair; "for I am not afraid of this Hermetrude either."

"But, to be sure, Hamlet, you are not afraid of her, at this distance. You have no cause to be afraid of her, so long as you keep out of her reach; and I rejoice, you must let me tell you, to see you so careful of your skin. In a newly married man, extreme prudence is highly becoming; and I do not for a moment think that, now you have proposed such noble plans, and then backed out of their execution, very many persons will be so uncivil as to find fault with your fear of going into Pictland. At any rate, they shall not make fun of you, openly, to your face, here in Deira," King Edric promised protectively. "I shall give explicit orders to my people that nothing of the sort is to be permitted. If behind your back they do laugh at you—oh, but just a little, Hamlet,—that can hurt nobody; and in due time you may live it down, perhaps."

"Confound my face! and my back too! and confound your notions of civility!" said Hamlet.

"Come, son-in-law, but let us not lose our tempers—!"

"I am not losing my temper," Hamlet cried out, as he dashed down his bronze goblet upon the floor with such vigor as to crush the cup out of shape. "To the contrary, I am asking you, in all calmness, do you or do you not want Queen Hermetrude as your seventh wife?"

"I want her very much"—the King of Deira conceded, as he looked, sidewise and with ruefulness, toward the floor,—"now that you have suggested this marriage and have so forcibly argued me into consenting to it. However, let us talk about other matters, since boldness has spilled out of you, like the ale from your goblet. That was one of my best goblets. It was sent to me, I must tell you, Hamlet, with five other goblets and a pair of gold-mounted drinking horns, by my poor lost friend, King Ethelred of Mercia. That was a good long while, of course, before he got corrupted with heresy, and became a Christian monk, down yonder in Rome. Such irreligious behavior, in public, upon the part of an English king"—Edric prattled on, relentlessly,—"was a great shock to me, Hamlet; so I am not defending it; quite the contrary; for that sort of thing sets a bad example; but I still value his goblets."

Hamlet spoke, with rancor, as to a place in which Edric could put every one of his goblets, so far as Hamlet cared; and Hamlet added,—

"I must get ready to go into Pictland."

The civility proper to a king could not hide the astonishment unavoidable in a father-in-law; but Edric remained firm.

"My dear Hamlet! I could not permit it. I admit frankly, since in these matters frankness is best, that you display more courage than I thought you possessed. Yet in this case something more than brute courage is required. You could not ever circumvent that woman in artfulness, any more than you could get the better of her in combat—"

Hamlet cried out: "I can do both. I will do both."

"But Hermetrude," said Edric, "is captain of the War Women of Mel. She is accounted the finest warrior of these times—"

Hamlet shouted: "I conquered Jutland unaided. I am better than she is."

"Nor would it have a good appearance, Hamlet, for you to be leaving your wife so soon after marriage—"

"It would have yet a worse appearance," said Hamlet ragingly, "for me to be permitting any such ugly reflections on my intelligence and my courage! and for me to have all your white-livered smug silly earls laughing at me behind my back!"

"Well, my dear boy," said Edric—with a relapse into the stoic tolerance of a relative by marriage,—"it may that you are right in not wishing people to make fun of you as a mere fool and a braggart. And so, for the sake of keeping clean your honor, I suppose I shall have to accept your offer, since you insist on it."

Edric smiled then, to observe how neatly he was getting rid of this bull-headed stupid Hamlet. In Pictland, Queen Hermetrude would dispose of him out of hand. Fengon would be avenged; and King Edric, without at all upsetting the routine of his home-life, would have kept faith as a foster-brother. Not many persons would have been shrewd enough, the King of Deira considered, to find a clear road to these benefits in gray Orton's simple-minded babble.

22

THE LOVE-MAKING OF FERBIS OF ABLACH

IT IS RELATED THAT UPON THE SAME MORNING during which Hamlet rode northward unaccompanied, Ferbis, the young Lord of Ablach, was trying to marry Queen Hermetrude, who ruled over Pictland and Mel and some part of Berwick. The manner of his courtship was thus:

First of all, into a field near the palace at Alcluid came the Queen's sister Estrild, armed in pale bronze, and fetching with her four poles of hazelwood. She drove these poles into the ground, so that they marked out a square space thirteen feet in length. In the centre of this square, Estrild spread out a white cloak which measured ten full paces from one end to the other end. At each corner of this cloak was a leather loop, by means of which the cloak was fastened down, among the new clover leaves, firmly and smoothly, with two pegs of oak-wood and with two pegs of ash-wood. This cloak was white in its color so that the first bloodstain to fall upon it would show the more clearly.

Estrild held each of her ear lobes between her

thumb and her fore-finger. At each peg she spread
out her legs; and bending downward, with the rapt
countenance of sincere piety, she gazed up between
her parted legs toward heaven and the gods that
had power over Pictland, while she was speaking
the formula of the peg sacrifice. So did Estrild
sanctify the place in which Ferbis wooed Hermetrude.

They entered this place armed. They stood
upon the cloak, facing each other, with their shields
up and their swords drawn. Hermetrude struck the
first blow, with her world-famous sword, called
Sleep-Giver. Ferbis parried death by means of his
very long narrow shield, which displayed a silver
unicorn, grazing, upon a red field. He attacked his
desired wife with the wild ardor of unbounded
affection, and he knocked her flatwise, so strong
was his love. She leaped nimbly to her feet, unhurt.
She split open his gilt helmet with a fierce stroke,
and Ferbis, reeling backward, quitted the white
cloak for an instant, but yet managing—just how,
he could not have said—to keep within the four
hazel posts. A retreat beyond those posts would
have meant the relinquishment of his love-making.

Now Ferbis assailed Hermetrude with a furious down-pour of blows struck almost at random.
Composedly, the large strong woman sliced away
a third part of his shield, beheading the unicorn.

Ferbis stepped backward. In that instant of his confusion, Hermetrude slashed his right hand, and blood dropped from it on the white cloak.

Queen Hermetrude said then: "By the rules of our gaming, Ferbis, you owe me three marks, and your life also. Do you pay me the twenty-four aurar first."

He obeyed. He knelt down before her.

Tall Hermetrude looked at him. She was quiet and serene, a little pensive, and wholly beautiful. The nostrils of her handsome high proud nose dilated; she breathed more deeply; her tongue moistened each corner of her lovely but generously proportioned mouth: otherwise the triumphant Queen did not move.

Young Ferbis touched reverently her knees. He noted, as dying men observe such trifles, that the sturdy legs of Hermetrude were wrapped about with broad thongs of deer skin; upon her feet were fine coverings made out of cow skin stained red. They were fastened with gilt strings. He noticed likewise that in the woods south of this field, a thrush was singing.

Ferbis wondered if thrushes could be mating thus late in the year? He remembered then that the doings of a thrush did not matter to Ferbis of Ablach. Nothing whatever would matter to Ferbis of Ablach—whoever he might be—after the instant now passing. Nothing, during this instant, mattered except the tall and not unfriendly woman who stood before him.

"To you who have had all I had to give," said Ferbis, "I give what alone remains. My restive dreams and hopes and desires have now ended; they fall away from me, like frail gray ashes, in the flame of your beauty. I am at peace, dear Queen; and I give praise to Heaven that I may quit this world seeing only what is most lovely in it and not needing any longer to think about anything else."

The Queen answered, "There is pity in my heart."

"But what of love?" says Ferbis.

"Why, but indeed I love you, and I love you alone, O very dear and foolish Ferbis,—at this moment."

"Then," said he gladly, "it is my will there should be no other moments."

She nodded in half-pleased assent. She bent down her lips to his hungry, searching, so young lips; and Queen Hermetrude said,—

"May the gods make smooth the dark path before you!"

"And you," replied Ferbis, smiling, "may you live safe from all harm forever. May the dark eyes before me not ever shed one tear."

Then Magnus the Skald struck off the head

of Ferbis of Ablach. And afterward, among a buzz of pleased comment—for the entire court of Pictland found a romantic interest in the truculent love-affairs of their Queen, and most of the noble persons who served her had hurried through breakfast, and were assembled in large numbers, to witness the latest of her wooings,—Queen Hermetrude returned to her palace.

The pensive executioner alone remained, beside the remnants of his deceased client. The glad thrush sang loudly and yet more loudly.

Said Magnus: "The Queen has brought you to a hard bed, O beautiful Ferbis, now that you rest upon stones and young clover, with the head cut away from your body. Your brown eyes that were friendly and generous are without sight; your heart that was filled with love does not exult any more; the hands that were nimble at wrestling and at harp-playing and at battle are folded in sleep. Your bed is mournful; it is not like the gilded and soft and purple-curtained bed of Hermetrude. Of the shining fighting-men in armor that gave you obedience, O beautiful Ferbis, and of the fond women who gave you their bodies, each now must raise a lamenting to see you enter the soiled bed of death."

Moreover Magnus said: "Death is that harlot with whom all men must sleep at last. From that which is good and wise and pleasant this ugly harlot draws us away with her foul cunning. All beauty, all power and all honor must lie down in her ignoble bed; they must give up their gloriousness forever, as the price of one cold kiss from the gray mouth of death. Even so do I kiss your lips, O very beautiful Ferbis, holding up your head between my two hands; and my grieving for you is greater than my lust. I have weighed the doings of applauded kings and of noted heroes and of yet other persons who got fame from out of a defeat of their human frailty before dark death ensnared them; and I find it is not decent for any man so openly to bestir himself, as did each one of these fine people, in earning this harsh whore's hire."

23

OF WIGLERUS: HOW HE FARED WITH A QUEEN

THAT QUEEN HERMETRUDE HATED THE IDEA OF any amorous intimacy, and was determined to remain always a virgin, was known upon the best possible authority, inasmuch as she said so herself. She spoke indeed of this hatred and of this determination to every noble person who came a-wooing; and added that, as was the approved custom of the War Women of Mel, she would submit her body to no man who could not conquer it.

Her fine looks, abetted by her great name and her notable riches, had spurred many heroes to attempt the task. Each one of these bold suitors Hermetrude had rejected, shyly but openly, through the same ceremonials in which Ferbis of Ablach had lost his head; and each one of them whom she did not happen to despatch during the hurly-burly of courtship had been attended to, a bit later, by Magnus.

So her promise yet stood: she would yield in marriage her hand, along with divers other parts of her body, to him who withstood the strength of her hand in battle, and who dejected, with no aid except only his sword, that fair but athletic body which few men could behold without desire, and none oppose without peril. And from all portions of earth, the young princes and kings and broad-shouldered champions trooped to besiege her maiden affections, each one of them riding gaily toward Alcluid in high hopes, and departing, if at all, in fragments. Such, very recently, had been the fate of Ferbis of Ablach, and of Heinrich the Red, and of Andrew of Lower Druim, and of Harold White-Tooth, and of Charles of Ardray, and of Osgar the Bishop-Margrave, and of René of Saz, and of Ralph Rough-Head of Lombardy, along with eight other princes of less fame but twin hardihood. Each one of these had ridden into Pictland to put, first, defeat, and after that, to put birth, upon Queen Hermetrude; but instead, upon all these she had put tombstones, even since Wiglerus came into Pictland.

"You have, in brief, a too impetuous nature,"—was the verdict of Wiglerus—"and it is not tactful to destroy so many bold men-at-arms simply because of their indiscretion in wishing to marry you."

"But I detest men—with, it is possible, just one exception, dear rogue," the Queen answered,—

"and I intend always to live at my own will, without having any jealous whining husband to interfere with it."

Said Wiglerus: "That is not quite the point; and I still think it would be more urbane of you to check the respectful ardors of a suitor by some method less drastic than killing him."

She looked at him, with her lips a little parted, as was the Queen's habit when in doubt or in meditation.

"Yet how, Wiglerus, can I help killing him? A virgin queen has to observe conventions or else be talked about most unfavorably. Beyond the most ancient memory of man and of man's variability it has been the custom of the War Women of Mel for every soldier to be conquered, in fair battle, openly, before she lets any husband put birth upon her. So I must either kill my lover or else let him conquer and marry me,—and then perhaps turn out a poor manager filling up all my castle here with his squalling babies and wasting my substance in his extravagance."

Wiglerus says, laughing: "Hark to the frugal Scotswoman! It is well that I at least did not approach you with any honorable intentions of marriage."

"I too am glad, dear rogue, that you behaved so very, very outrageously. In battle I would have to kill you for the sake of my honor. But in bed it is different."

"In fact"—Wiglerus philosophized—"honor does not intrude between the bed-spread and the mattress. And just as you say, Hermetrude, in a lectual skirmish, the strategy and the methods of attack, the recruiting of forces and the weapons employed and the final entry into the besieged place, are not always entrusted to an infirm general in chief attended by his staff of lieutenants and his military band."

"But, I did not say that," the Queen pointed out.

"Why should you?" he replied. "What possible doubt as to the marked difference can exist between us, after last night, and after the night before, and after yet a number of other blissful occasions?"

Hermetrude answered, with the remorse of a correctly reared gentlewoman who has been dishonored without being detected:

"That I have been indiscreet is true. And I simply do not know what I could have been thinking about!"

"Neither of us was thinking at all, my dear," he assured her. "We were enraptured very far beyond rationality. That is the main, if it indeed be not the sole, charm of all such undignified exercises."

"But do you respect me as much as ever, Wiglerus? And do you not feel that, just for the moment, we were both swept off our feet, as it were, by the force of a passion so strong as to be beyond our control?"

"No," Wiglerus replied; "and neither do you. Yet thus, I have no least doubt, the hen talks to the cock when she gets up and shakes herself,—and the cow to the bull, and even the lioness to the lion; for to my experience, there is no feminine creature anywhere who does not append to the carnal comedy just that same epilogue which you are now speaking."

"Still, it sounds a great deal better to feel that way," said Hermetrude. "So we ought to. And for the rest, dear rogue, do you indeed love me as you have not loved any woman before? for it is that, after all, which makes the difference."

"Alas, my darling," said Wiglerus, "but I am not any longer in the first prodigal flowering of my youth. And so, no matter what at heart may be the warmth of my mature adoration, in displaying it, where once I was hasty and awkward, and perhaps over-repetitious, I now affect a more polite reticence; I avoid sloth as well as parsimony, I believe: yet I stay at pains to remember that any supreme outburst of affection should be perfectly timed—

let us say—with the responsiveness of my companion."

"I did not mean that at all, you lewd scoffer; nor do I at all understand what you are talking about. I think it is much nicer, of course; yet you speak of courtesies which a truly modest unmarried woman prefers to appreciate in silence rather than to discuss. No, Wiglerus: I mean, do you love me to-day as much as you once loved Alftruda?"

"I find you wholly charming," he stated.

Then Hermetrude spoke sharply. Wiglerus noted that the pupils of her large brown eyes had contracted oddly, and that her eyes seemed more pale in color. Her eyes now were tinted like amber.

"And yet," says she, "there is the memory of Alftruda between us always. You thrust it aside. You defy it in order that you may approach me. You content your leisurely and stinted and half-feminine lust with the aid of my body. With the aid of my body you get your piddling refinements of hoggishness, you get your desired drunkenness of oblivion, for a little while. Then always, Wiglerus, that memory of Alftruda comes back, bringing with it a dislike of yourself and contempt for Hermetrude. You do not then regain instantly your cool perky self-conceit, nor your mild feeling of friendliness—for the Queen of Pictland!"

Wiglerus now considered his quite handsome

and highly indignant companion with a pleased interest.

"My dear," he said soberly, "you have far more perceptiveness than I thought. I apologize. Yet do you rest assured that in the mind of any man who ever makes love to you satisfyingly there must harbor some such memory. That is unavoidable. A man may share his laughter and his affections, and his body likewise, with many women. His heart he can give to but one woman, once and forever. He does not usually win that woman, because under the influence of sincere passion a lover figures to the worst possible advantage; and in fact he becomes a mere idiot with whom no sane woman would encumber her household. So she prefers somebody else; and to the man who has given her his heart she, in exchange, can give only unhappiness. Thus, for a while at any rate, does it appear. Yet how utterly does her discarded, miserable and thrice-fortunate lover, by-and-by, perceive his delusion, when he fancied himself to have been luckless! Now that his heart is given away, once and for all, it cannot any longer blunder into his heart-affairs; their management has been taken over by his head; and under this new régime they afford him a never fluctuating income of diversion. He has become incapable of caring about any woman beyond the dictates of convenience: such is his tuition fee in the fine art of love-making. And it is only through making this down payment, my dear Hermetrude, that any man may ever hope to become forever afterward a satisfying lover for all women—except only the one woman he wants,—because whether he wins or loses in the game which he is playing does not any longer matter to him."

"So!" says the Queen,—and she quitted her purple-curtained bed, without ceremony, because of her anger to hear voiced any such degraded sentiments.

Wiglerus in this way was left alone between the rumpled pink sheets, with a queen glaring down at him in unrestrained maidenly indignation; yet anger and ferocity and all other acrid emotions were very becoming to Hermetrude, the recumbent virtuoso decided, for they gave to her a vivacity and a sparkle which her amorous moments lacked. In brief, he now found her to be peculiarly handsome, —and the more so because it happened that, at the instant, Hermetrude was not wearing anything except a silver bag fastened to her right knee, in which bag this Scottish queen carried at all times her more valuable gems.

"So, you spruce grinning lecher," the Queen shouted; "and do you think any proper-spirited woman can be contented by your damned

Alftruda's leavings! What do you think a woman is! or do you believe me a mere idiot!"

"Since you have put the question," said Wiglerus, "I will answer it. A woman is an orifice with more or less pleasant surroundings. That these now and then embrace a superb brain, more free of prejudice and far better balanced than is any masculine brain, I would be the most insistent of all living persons to assert, if but out of politeness. So do you laugh and lie down," says Wiglerus, as he continued to regard the incensed young sovereign with a sturdy rise of approval. "That is an old saying; but I will now show you there is good sense in it. Here is your pillow. I do not think I ever slept with a more disorderly queen."

Afterward he went on, with an expression of undisturbed friendliness:

"To Alftruda I once gave my sincere worship, which bored the poor child rather unmercifully; and upon occasions I still devote to her some moody reflections and poetic yearnings, of which, by the best of luck, she remains unconscious. She would consider them, in connection with my own niece by marriage, to be not at all proper. But upon you, my dear Hermetrude,—by whom correctness is more valued in deportment than in private—hour after hour I squander the delights of my intimacy, the sparkle of my wit, the beauties of my personality, the charm of my affection, and the fond fervor of my caresses. It appears to me that yours is, by long odds, the better bargain."

"You talk; and you talk well enough," said Hermetrude, as she nestled back beside Wiglerus, half sullenly: "but you still love Alftruda. I do not love Alftruda."

24

OF HERMETRUDE: HER SELF-RESPECT: WHY SHE KILLED FIVE OF HER BOND-MEN

THAT HERMETRUDE IN ALL HER GREAT-SOULED nature had not one ounce of jealousy was a fact upon which, nowadays, she reflected with some insistence. The notable, and indeed the world-famous, Queen of Pictland had no need to be jealous of a two-penny Princess of Deira, whom her own husband (as entire Britain knew and repeated with relish) had exposed to derision as the granddaughter of a stable groom. It was only that Hermetrude was accustomed to being loved by desperate persons who, finding in her the woman of all youth's dreams, and a beauty beyond verbal description, were enslaved by passion; and who for the sake of her dear perfections sought out death smilingly. Because of Hermetrude, in dozens upon dozens of lands, and in all places where the brave loved nobly, men had put aside, as unvalued trifles, their wealth and their famousness and their broad kingdoms and even (as it was, of course, sad to recall) the clinging arms of their heart-broken wives, in exchange for bleak ruin, so bright and so fatal was the beauty of this virgin queen who had not—as everybody, with any good taste, noticed at once—her twin upon earth.

Very well, then! All that Hermetrude got from Wiglerus was a quiet sort of critical and half-negligent liking. She doubted if for her sake he would as much as postpone dinner. So his bland condescensions enraged her, even in the instant that she evoked them assiduously, the young Queen could not quite say why, except that this nimble, shrivelled, quizzical, ageing gentleman did (as people phrased it) have a way with him. Some day she would end by killing the Prince of Denmark, she was certain; she would have to do it, by-and-by, out of mere self-respect: and when that happened, it would all be the fault of that damned Alftruda. When you considered affairs rightly, it was Alftruda, and no other person, who had led the old pot-bellied popinjay into trifling with the peace of mind and even with the royal person of a virgin sovereign—or at any rate (the Queen corrected her meditations), of a practically virgin sovereign—in her own palace.

From such reflections Queen Hermetrude was roused by news that the King of Deira had become a suitor for her hand in marriage; and all pensiveness went away from her.

"You bring good hearing," said Hermetrude. "I shall deal lovingly with the crowned stable boy, out of my consideration for his family. Let Sleep-Giver be sharpened."

It was answered: "King Edric woos by proxy. He has sent as his proxy his son-in-law, the new King of Jutland."

"Select five of my bondmen—such as are a little past their work," said the Queen thriftily,—"and this afternoon we will sacrifice them to Odin; for the gods smile upon Pictland. And do you let Sleep-Giver be thrice sharpened, now that Alftruda's husband and dear love is at hand to try conclusions with me."

Hermetrude went out with flushed eagerness. She stayed only to put on a white kirtle figured with gold, and over it a scarlet cloak patterned richly with gold lace even down to the skirt. As befitted a maiden queen, she left unconfined her lovely, gleaming, but rather short, brown hair, which fell only to her shoulders; but about her forehead she placed a gold band inset with garnets. No living male creature except a lapidary, the Scottish Queen reflected, could ever distinguish between them and real rubies.

She came thus to destroy Hamlet; and upon seeing him, paused. Enraged Hermetrude did not speak at once, although her somewhat large mouth remained open. It was then a wonder to note how ferocity ebbed and gave way to quite another expression, because at her first glimpse of this burly blond giant, the Queen knew that her sword, Sleep-Giver, was not destined to subdue Hamlet.

25

OF HERMETRUDE: HOW SHE PUNISHED PLEASANTLY

WE MUST TELL HOW THE QUEEN OF THE PICTS embraced her cousin and good friend of Jutland, kissing him upon both cheeks. She said, with a combining of humility and of admiration which she, very plainly, was trying to conceal,—

"I had never looked for any happiness so complete as to be saluting as my guest that great Prince of the North who has made himself famous and dreadful, throughout all the nations of the world, by his unexampled exploits."

"You speak rather too generously," replied Hamlet. "It is not in my own person, nor in the splendor of my own doings, I approach you. They may, or they may not, have been notable. I prefer not to say. But people do, of course, talk about them. You know how people are, even people of eminence. I had, in fact, no great while ago, a letter from the Emperor of Almaine which you might perhaps find of interest. He said, ah, but quite a number of handsome things. From a monarch in his position, that letter would have pleased anybody. I must show you that letter. However!" —and Hamlet checked, with abruptness, the on-flow of egotism—"I do not come to you as a person whom the world is discussing. I come as the ambassador of the King of Deira."

"So I had heard—O all-glorious and far too modest Hamlet,—with some doubtfulness. I am grateful"—the Queen declared, flushing in tender rapture—"to the person who sent you hither, no matter what might be his reason. Yet I marvel that the renowned soothsayer of Middleburgh and the superb hero of Sundby should have become the errand boy of an imposter so base in quality and so beggared in reputation as is Edric of Deira."

—Which sounded quite nicely, to the Queen's taste. But the hopes of this special gambit she now saw to have been obscured by a sullen frown.

"You forget one matter," said Hamlet. "You forget you speak of my father-in-law."

"I speak," Hermetrude returned with spirit, "of that age-frozen usurper whom your own penetration discovered, and whom your intrepid plain-speaking has denounced to all Britain, as the bastard of a stable groom."

Hamlet said: "What man can prevent or alter his own begetting? King Edric is my wife's father. That contents me."

Impulsively, Queen Hermetrude touched the large hairy hand of Hamlet, with a light and cordial gesture.

"My dear lord! but let us speak with that frankness which befits royal persons. Upon the painful theme of your wife, as you call her—with a ready tactfulness in speech which I appreciate— it is perhaps better for a virgin queen not to harp. In consequence I shall not harp. I remark merely that you and I are not baseborn. You are a king inferior to no prince in Europe for the antiquity of your blood and the nobility of your exploits, nor for that matter—as you must permit me to tell you with bluntness—for the handsomeness of your person. I am a queen, in my own right, over no little kingdom. It is suitable that we two, who were not spawned in a hayloft, should deal with each other in complete honesty."

Hamlet replied: "Say what you will, O most lovely of all living queens. Even though you were to talk nonsense, yet the rich music of your voice would delight me."

Under this permission, Hermetrude made clear her desire to speak with all charity of this woman whom Hamlet had described as his wife—through an excess of great-heartedness, and of forgiveness for the injuries he had suffered, to which Hermetrude, because of one's need not to embarrass her cousin of Jutland, would not attempt to give the praise it deserved. She would say only that the young woman—though indeed, Hermetrude had forgotten the poor creature's name—

Hamlet answered, "She is called Alftruda."

And that, said Hermetrude graciously, was truly a very pretty name. Well, and this Elfrida—

Hamlet said, "Alftruda."

Why, but yes, to be sure, said Hermetrude; and this Ethelburga was no doubt wholly beautiful. Yet could Hamlet be so unthinking as to forget that a king's marriage should not be prompted by any foolish weighing of outward shaping and colors, but rather by such virtues and antiquity of race as would cause his wife to be honored, and to be accepted, by the great Emperor Charles of Almaine, for example, as a fit mate for Hamlet? Exterior graces were as nothing where perfections of mind and character, and the purity of an unstained conscience, did not accompany and adorn that which was seen externally. Upon the question, and in fact the somewhat embarrassing question, whether or not this Torfrida—

Hamlet said, "Alftruda."

Really, said Hermetrude, but those dreadful Saxon names were beyond belief! Of course, though, in a country where the queen spent her nights in the stable, one could not hope for very much in the way of refinement. And if you did inherit, from your own grandmother, a tendency to such lewdness, why, it might, just now and then, prove too strong for you. One ought to be charitable in considering these cases of morbid and depraved lust. So without saying anything at all about it, Hermetrude preferred to dismiss the highly distasteful question, whether or not this Alftruda had been the mistress of Prince Wiglerus before she married Hamlet—

"Hah!" says Hamlet.

—Because, Hermetrude continued, almost any ignorant, half barbarian girl would be as wax under the artfulness of a seducer so experienced. The girl would not really be much to blame. The fornications of Alftruda, no matter how regrettable they might have been, nor just how many men were concerned in them, were not the point. The point was that Hamlet ought to think twice before condoning Alftruda's lack of chastity, and of some proper self-control, simply on account of Alftruda's good looks. The good looks of a deceiving hussy had misled many other heroes of distinction before to-day, like enticing baits which lured onward these champions until they were cast headlong into dark gulfs of ruin and dishonor, like King Agamemnon of Athens, and King Sisera of Harosheth, and King Antony of Egypt. Hermetrude then mentioned yet a few other potentates and captains, and a half-dozen outstanding philosophers, whom misplaced love had drawn to destruction.

"Now' but indeed," said Hamlet, "if any of these outlandish harlots had learning such as I am listening to, I do not doubt their seductiveness. If they had as much beauty as I am looking at, I do not think their bedfellows were altogether to be pitied."

But from these dicta Queen Hermetrude dissented. Neither the extent of her quite limited education nor, most certainly, her own poor exterior was the point at issue. The point was that the entire civilized world now wondered that, in spite of these dreadful exemplary warnings which she had cited, the son of King Horvendile, and the grandson of King Rörek Slyngebond, after having so valiantly overcome the malevolence and the wicked subtleties of King Fengon, should himself be overcome by Alftruda; and that the same Hamlet who had risen so high at the trumpet call of filial duty should now abase himself at the lewd whisper of carnal lust. Hermetrude herself would not say—as it appeared her mere friendly duty to inform her cousin of Jutland, so very, very many persons were saying everywhere—that Hamlet thus publicly bartered his honor in order to get what Wiglerus, and perhaps a few other men, had not cared to keep, because people did often exaggerate matters of this kind, without stopping to think that Wiglerus, who liked variety, would hardly have spent more than a night or two with Alftruda. People ought not to stretch the truth in this way. People ought to be more charitable. And because of these considerations, Hermetrude could declare merely, with every sort of proper restraint, that the world marvelled to see one who in excellence and wisdom and valor had seemed to surpass the topmost exploits of humankind now stooping so low as to consort, openly, with a debauched descendant of horse grooms and chambermaids, when it was the plain duty of a King of Jutland to keep safe the power of Jutland.

Hamlet grunted, "How?"

"Why, but, in this most unfortunate instance, through divorce, to begin with," says Hermetrude; "and after that"—she glanced downward, the confused and helpless prey of an inexperienced maid's modesty and of fond hopes which she, it was evident, did not dare utter—"through some suitable royal alliance."

"I think you are right," said Hamlet.

He had colored under the grave sweetness of Hermetrude's rebuke to his wanton behavior, and under the tenderness of her inspiring appeal to the more lofty side of his nature; but he spoke now, in his everyday abrupt fashion, calmly enough, with remorse. He conceded that, out of plain decency, he ought to have married after a fashion more helpful to Jutland and better calculated to impress favorably the Emperor of Almaine. Kings, Hamlet admitted, in such matters as marriage, ought to be unselfish. Kings should piously restrict gross carnal indulgence to irregular love-affairs. Hamlet rejoiced that, even so, it stayed possible for him to atone. He would pronounce a divorce in the presence of witnesses. He would thus get rid forever of the young strumpet at the present instant disgracing the throne of Jutland. He would have no further dealings with this servant girl, who had misled Hamlet into unkingly conduct and the contempt of right-thinking persons.

"—After which," Hamlet continued, "I intend to marry you. I like the wisdom and the gentle charitableness of your speaking. I like your book knowledge. I like also the bright colors of your body, dear lady of Pictland. So it is my need to conquer you after the honorable custom of your country."

"Ah, but that seems to me a foolish, and in fact, a very dangerous old custom," replied Hermetrude—"now."

"Why?" says Hamlet.

"—Because, O king of all men," she explained,

with fond, if reluctant, candor, "your opponent would be an enfeebled creature whom the divine power of love has already conquered."

At that, Hamlet arose from the bench they were sitting on. He closed both the doors to the room. He said then:

"Love has overcome both of us. For us to be fighting each other with swords would be silly. So let us try other weapons," he remarked jovially; and he pinched her leg, just as aforetime he had pinched the leg of Alftruda.

"You ought," said Hermetrude, without any special conviction, "to be ashamed of yourself."

Neither one of them spoke, after that, for an appreciable while.

Then, by-and-by, Hermetrude said: "But I should not have given in to you so easily. I should not have been thus frank with you, at our very first meeting; and I simply do not know what I could have been thinking about! Hamlet, are you quite sure that you respect me as much as ever?"

"Oh, but ten thousand thousand times much more, my darling," he sighed gustily.

"And do you not feel, dear lord, that just for the moment we have been swept off our feet, as it were, by the force of a naughty passion so strong as to be beyond our control?"

"Such is my exact feeling," he replied with

astonishment, "and it is uncanny, the way in which you read my thoughts."

"Why, then it is perhaps best, my adored Hamlet,—after you have divorced that unfortunate creature, for whom I have only pity and no more contempt than is unavoidable—for you to accept, not as the prize of battle, but as a free gift, my hand in marriage, along with my poor ravished body and my conquered heart."

"What man is there, unless he be made of stone, or of soured milk curds, or of complete ice," tall Hamlet demanded, of the palace ceiling, "who would refuse such gifts?"

"My dear lord," replied Hermetrude, smoothing down her very best white kirtle into tidiness— and noting, with a thrifty disfavor, that during the interview just concluded it had been ripped in two places,—"I rejoice we agree thus happily. I am sure, from what I now know of you, that the demonstrations of your regard will remain deep and lively for years to come. Of my own devoted love I prefer—in my present confused state of unexampled rapture and of not inexcusable embarrassment,—to say nothing. Yet do you now receive as your Queen one who, within the length of a day, will bestow upon you far more of contentment and of honor than that draggle-tail little Princess of Deira could ever give to anybody in a lifetime."

In this way was the affair concluded. And upon the wide lips of Hermetrude rested a well practised smile of adoring tenderness; in her plump cheeks the excitement of this touch-and-go game had sketched a quite neat replica of the fond flush of first love: but in her Scots mind harbored a cool joy over the inexpensive manner in which she had disposed of Hamlet, and of Alftruda, and of old Wiglerus too, all at the same instant, and rather pleasantly than otherwise.

26

WHY WIGLERUS WENT SOUTH

Now GRAY ORTON SAT HOLDING UPRIGHT HIS cane of carved orange-wood between his gray knees, as he gazed upon Wiglerus, consideringly, with a compassionate benevolence.

"—For you. position, my dear Prince," Orton resumed, "is one of extreme delicacy; and we confront a situation in which, I submit, you cannot afford idleness."

"I agree with you," said Wiglerus, "since it appears that, after taking away from me the Alftruda whom I loved, my nephew is now taking likewise the Hermetrude who amused me; and that he plans also to take my life. The acquisitiveness of this bull-headed young man begins, I admit, to become an active nuisance."

Orton replied: "Indeed, but you would do well to express your disapproval of his unkinsmanlike conduct by leaving Pictland, because otherwise both Hamlet and Hermetrude intend to have you killed."

"I can see the need of that from the lady's

point of view," returned Wiglerus, with unflagging urbanity, "inasmuch as I know too much about Hermetrude for a maiden queen's comfort. Nor of course does the considerate person expect decent behavior of a woman with whom he has prospered in tender relations. Against Hermetrude I can bear no grudge. Even Hamlet, so far as goes my mere murder, is exercising the inalienable privilege of a Nordic gentleman to kill any other Nordic gentleman whose existence has become inconvenient. No, Orton: I am willing to be broad-minded about murder—but not about unfaith. Hamlet has the right to divorce his wife, if he desires thus grossly to offend her virtue and his own interests; that my long-legged nephew should provoke for himself ruin through breaking an oath made to Heaven, is an affair with which I lack concern; but I cannot in honor permit anybody to break an oath made to me. The big sprawling young goat was explicit. 'If ever my faith fails her,' says he, in his gold-figured tunic, to me in my poor nakedness, 'then let my head answer for it.' On that agreement I shake hands; on that agreement I will shake worlds. Because of this cut-throat whore he has cast out Alftruda, into the gutter. Alftruda!"

Wiglerus cried out the name wailingly. He crashed down both hands upon the table beside him, with so great violence that his well-tended hands, when he lifted them in a polite gesture of apology, were both bleeding. Upon his cheeks you saw tears, but the man's thin lips smiled affably.

"You must pardon me, Orton: I love Alftruda. Very well, then! This Hamlet is a king, I am nobody; he is young, I am somewhat sunk in age; in brief, he has all, and I have nothing: but I mean to lop off his fine, handsome, empty head, none the less, if only because I do not care to have my own nephew break faith. Hamlet shall keep his oath to me."

Orton said only, with unruffled beneficence, "Why, but of course you can get his head, Wiglerus, if you desire it, and are willing to pay for it properly."

"I stand ready to barter my soul for it, Orton."

Over that notion Orton could not hide his amusement.

"My dear Wiglerus," says he, "even if I had come to you infernally accredited—as you appear to imagine, upon grounds unknown to me,—yet common honesty would forbid any self-respecting fiend, at this special instant, to close the bargain you offer. No, Wiglerus: I at least do not swindle my friends; I am, first and always, a romanticist who is not satisfied by the unimaginative manner in which Heaven conducts the affairs of this world; and you mortal romanticists are a great aid to me.

So for no price at all, do you consider this crystal which I am now taking out of my bosom, because of my natural kindness."

Wiglerus looked at the crystal, which was about the shape and the size of an orange; and he said, with half-rueful amusement:

"In Strasburg, in the street of the jewel dealers, when I was younger, I once saw such a trinket. It had lain buried for nine weeks upon the face of a dead man, so its owner told me; and in a place where no cock had ever crowed or any bell sounded, he invoked three spirits. Afterward I observed, in that other crystal, the doings of a Flemish gentlewoman with whom I was then in love; and I was so cured of my love."

"Oh, but yes; for you dealt then with Ariel and Marbuel and Aciel," replied Orton. "They are competent; and indeed, in their own small way, they are quite reliable. I say nothing against the poor devils. But this crystal is different. It is, as it were, a souvenir of my own youth. It is a bit of jasper stone broken off from the city gate of a rather gaudy seaside resort which I left before the place became overrun with Christians; and this scrying-stone has been laid, for only three weeks, in nothing more remarkable than water in which the first-born son of a king had been bathed, by an insane Baptist prophet, down in Palestine. Nothing is hid from this scrying-stone, be it in field or in forest or afloat, be it master or mistress or servant, be it for good or for wickedness or for compromise, as you may now see."

Wiglerus looked; and in the depths of the crystal he observed a confused moving of small figures.

"They carry a dead man," says Wiglerus. "He has a reddish streaked white beard and a huge hooked nose with which I am not unfamiliar."

"In Denmark," Orton answered, "King Rörek Slyngebond goes to his last rest."

"And so," said Wiglerus, with some gravity, "my father is dead. I am sorry; and I regret too that —on account of Helga, I believe it was,—his last words to me were of a distinctly comminatory nature. Yes, I am sorry; yet I never quite got on with him after he strangled my mother; and besides that, all the persons whom I loved in boyhood have died or left me, or else they have hurt me in some way or another which taught me to beware of very deep emotion."

It was a rule of conduct which Orton endorsed with a nod of alert approval. Orton then explained,—

"Your father is dead, Wiglerus, because your elder brother Einar has smothered the infirm old

[166]

sea-robber while he lay ill abed; and in his place rules Einar."

"Indeed," said Wiglerus, "we Harfaagers are not wholly admirable in our family relations; for I quite readily believe any sort of evil about any one of my kindred. But in this crystal the small puppet show changes. I now see that big black-browed Einar goes crowned, and some three-fourths tipsy, into a church, where two bishops lead him to the King's seat on the north side of the choir. My brother Thorfin sits next to the King. He lays his hand upon Einar's shoulder, and I behold a wonder; for with those bitter lips which no kindness has ever touched, lean Thorfin speaks amicably."

Says Orton: "Your brother Thorfin is admiring the fine purple cloak which your brother Einar wears in honor of this festival. Your brother Thorfin is making sure that under this finery the new King of Denmark does not wear armor."

Then Wiglerus said: "My brother Einar stands before the altar. He holds up both hands above his head, and he bows down before the altar, praising Odin the Lord of Spears, the Father of Ages, the Loving One, the Preserver of King Einar. Thorfin strikes now, from behind, with a long knife."

"And he strikes handsomely," said Orton. "He delivers with some emphasis that knife-stroke which makes Thorfin King over all Denmark."

"I think not," Wiglerus answered; "for do you not see how Einar staggers upward to his feet, and turns about in his customary vile temper? Come, but this puppet show quickens in action! It is not Einar who has been killed. Instead, it is Einar who is giving orders. His men have obeyed these orders. Because of these orders I can now see, in lean Thorfin's place, only that which five battle-axes have left of Thorfin."

Wiglerus gulped. He then said, with an urbane smiling:

"The residuum is ugly. It is like a lump of raw sprawling quivering red pulp."

"It is the same flesh as your flesh, Wiglerus: but do you regard Einar."

Wiglerus, white to the lips, but otherwise not showing any inurbane emotion, replied:

"Einar has watched all. He has looked on, without any movement, like a brooding buzzard, while his men made mincemeat out of Thorfin. Now dark Einar sits alone in the King's seat. His hands clasp his right side. Between his fingers oozes blood."

"And that blood is the same as your blood, Wiglerus," said Orton, pensively.

He looked at Wiglerus, for some while, with approval. He continued:

"Meanwhile, it is as I told you. Thorfin struck

very mightily, straight through the lungs of huge Einar. You should be grateful to Thorfin, inasmuch as because of him there is no need to barter your soul. Now that King Einar dies, what is there to prevent you—O King Wiglerus," said Orton, with a smile of bedazzling amiability,—"from taking the head of Hamlet?"

Wiglerus answered, slowly closing and unclosing his long fingers:

"If this be a true seeming, then by inheritance I am King of Denmark. Yes, Orton: the peripeteia would be well contrived, if only I could trust your magic; for young Hamlet would be my vassal, holding his province and all his other belongings at my sole pleasure."

"Upon the faith of a proverbially famous gentleman," said Orton, "this is a true seeming. My scrying-stone does not lie; and in Denmark a throne awaits your taking."

"Then beyond question," replied Wiglerus, "it seems a large pity that at this special instant I lack the time to accept a throne. I cannot go into Denmark now. I must go to Alftruda."

Orton considered this saying with benign surprise; he turned his cane about meditatively, as he remarked:

"I have long cherished an admiring regard for your qualities, my poor Wiglerus; and among them until to-day I had ranked as invaluable your complete cool selfishness. To-day I am at a loss."

"To-day, friend Orton, you are not in love," said Wiglerus. "It is just that which makes the difference."

"I have been concerned in a few love-affairs," said Orton, musingly, "and yet—I admit it, Wiglerus,—I am not familiar with love as a passion which has much colored my own judgment. So it may be through inexperience, and because of my uneventful life, that I find it strange you should think a not very remarkable girl to be of more worth than is a kingdom as fine as Denmark."

"My intelligence assures me," returned Wiglerus, "that I behave with unheard-of foolishness. But my heart tells me, over and yet over again, with the smug malignity of a martyr under well merited persecution, that Alftruda needs my aid, because her husband and her father are now bound one of them to kill the other. Alftruda has need of me; against the welfare of Alftruda I would not weigh forty kingdoms: and so there is not any more to be said."

"But I," replied Orton, "I say this much,— that men continue, even nowadays, to surprise even me. Do what one may, there is no civilizing the creatures; and the most unlikely of them are apt, at any moment, to develop a rude generosity of spirit. Yet that is curable."

"What means your riddle?" asked Wiglerus.

"I mean only that by-and-by," said Orton, "each one of you comes to a graveyard."

"That, Orton, is a truism; and truisms are destructive swords which ruin all freedom of thought."

"You speak truly, my dear over-gallant Wiglerus; and for that reason, every truism is double-edged," replied Orton.

Thus speaking, he departed rather suddenly for a crippled person. It was almost as if the gray man had vanished.

Wiglerus shrugged. Then Wiglerus rode southward, upon his dandelion-colored stallion, without saying good-by to anybody at Alcluid. When Hamlet learned of this, so great was his desire to have with him his uncle up to the hour of his uncle's death that Hamlet sent five Pictish assassins to pursue Wiglerus; but the as yet uncrowned King of Denmark got away safely, as far as Tunsberg, and into an old graveyard beyond Vagar.

27

STILL OF WIGLERUS: WHY HE STAYED IN THE GRAVEYARD

THE STORY SAYS THAT IN A GRAVEYARD, BUT A half-mile south of Vagar, Wiglerus met with a young woman who had on a cloak of two colors, black and white, as she came out of one of the vaults; and the tale also relates how greatly the appearance of this shining horseman, in that quiet place, startled her.

"I thought you were a robber," she declared. "But for an accident I encountered some while ago, you might have frightened me to death. I was never so startled in my life. Feel how my heart beats."

"On the contrary," said Wiglerus, out of his kindly desire to banish alarm, "I am merely a prince who rides abroad in search of diverting adventures; and I rob no woman of anything which she does not surrender of her own will."

"I am honored to encounter your Highness," said the lady, lifting up her eyebrows in the same instant that she closed the bosom of her white kirtle; "and your coming is strangely agreeable to me, whom the jealousy and the unworthy suspicions of an aged husband have brought to this dreary resting-place of the dead, where I am not permitted to see, except quite privately, any man except him."

Said gallant Wiglerus: "Yet your eyes are sapphires; your hair is thrice burnished gold; and your teeth I perceive to be thirty-two pearls of unequalled brilliancy. So do you tell me the name of the miser who would hide away so many valuable treasures unseen in a desolate graveyard. I will at once set you free of him."

"The infirmities of his age have already done that," the young lady answered. "No less a personage than Time, that august, if incontinent, begetter of all gods, has countersigned our divorce. I suffer no least inconvenience from my husband nowanights. And during the day time he talks. That is all."

She sighed, never so slightly.

"Merely to talk is not a proof of sincere affection," Wiglerus agreed. "It is through noble deeds that the love of a tender-hearted and healthy young woman must be retained."

The fair strange lady was now smiling up at him, very radiantly, with frank hopefulness.

"My health," she observed, "in spite of an incident which many physicians consider deadly, remains robust."

"And what of your heart, dear lady?" says Wiglerus, smiling back at one whom he perceived to be no unskilled player at the game which the two of them had in mind.

"My heart is not formed of granite," she admitted, "as I have noticed during the last two minutes. That is why, your Highness,—should you condone the frankness of a quite simply reared country gentlewoman—I would like you to stop talking; for upon my word, I have begun to mistake you for my husband."

Thereupon the same Wiglerus who had put by a kingdom because of his love for Alftruda dismounted from his dandelion-colored stallion, saying:

"And I, O most naïve and most adorable of living creatures, during the last two minutes, I have noticed you have beauty in your person, and intelligence in your mind, as well as—or so at least I suspect—both vivacity and an appetite in yet other quarters. No virtuoso of women would ask more."

"Indeed, your Highness," she replied, taking his hand shyly, "I believe that a true virtuoso would not ask at all."

"No," said Wiglerus; "for the virtuoso offends silently, and apologizes, with a proper degree of rhetoric, afterward. Yet since my coming had frightened you—"

"I am still frightened," she replied, guiding his hand. "Feel how my heart beats."

Five minutes later the lady, who had now put aside her black and white cloak, assured him that a virtuoso had no least need to apologize. So Wiglerus spent the night there, among tombstones, quite agreeably.

That was how the five Pictish murderers were enabled to overtake Wiglerus, and to capture him the next morning, while he lay asleep in a graveyard. The young woman had quitted him during the night, taking with her his purse, so that Wiglerus did not immediately find out her name, nor was it until a while later, at Thorë, that he saw her again. Meantime, his captors conveyed him northward, toward Botsuane, where fighting had begun between the Picts and the Deiri.

28

THE FIGHTING AT STRAITHKELD

IT IS TOLD THAT TO THE FINDING OF KING EDRIC, a war was inevitable after the King learned how his son-in-law had got from Queen Hermetrude not death but marriage. All Edric's plans had been upset; and his moral duty, to dispose mortally of the person who had killed Edric's foster-brother, remained undischarged.

The King of Deira, let it be remarked, had been patient beyond ordinary. He had not liked Hamlet's tediousness, in making public the irregularity of Edric's birth (about which Edric had known perfectly well since early childhood), but he had pardoned the tactless announcement of this shocking news, inasmuch as no large harm had come of it save only the rebelling of Morcar and Ethelwulf, whom he had executed with zest, and indeed with some active enjoyment. He was ready, in his own private reflections, to pardon the atrocious conduct of Hamlet in stealing Edric's intended bride, because at no price would Edric ever have married the termagant. And he could pardon also the fact

that Hamlet was now returning toward Middleburgh in order to divorce the daughter of Edric.
That, in some aspects, was an additional affront:
but then, to the other side, to do this was Hamlet's
unquestioned right; moreover, King Edric himself
had got rid of two wives in just this facile legal
manner, by pronouncing a divorce where they
could hear his voice in the presence of witnesses;
and besides that, in order to return to Deira, Hamlet would attempt to come through the pass of
Botsuane. Nothing could be more convenient.

Edric, in brief, had pardoned much. But he
could not honorably pardon the death of his foster-brother, or permit it to remain unavenged,
now that Hermetrude had cheated all rational expectations. So to begin with, he reprobated the
variability of women, which was forcing him to
do his own work. After that, he spoke with Alftruda; he sent out the war arrow, to get together
his army; and he laid an ambuscade where the main
road between Deira and Pictland went through the
pass of Botsuane.

The south end of this pass King Edric filled
up with boulders. The ground he sprinkled with
calthrops, so as to incommode the advance of in-
fantry and to check utterly all horsemen. He hid
his men-at-arms upon each side of the pass, behind
the lower trees of each steeply ascending hill-side;

and upon the higher cliffs he stationed his archers. An army which entered that narrow valley would find the way blocked before it, while death descended from each side, dealt by invisible enemies who remained beyond reach. There would be for that army no hope except only the lean mercy of swift destruction.

Here Edric waited. He grinned happily when he saw the Pictish army and the War Women of Mel and three lightly armed troops of Caledonians all coming toward his trap without any suspicion. At their head rode Hamlet and Hermetrude, both very handsomely mounted, upon white stallions, and agleam in gold-figured armor.

So they approached Botsuane and their destruction. The well hidden army of the Deiri watched all from the pine-wooded ridges and made ready for an easy massacre. Then waiting Edric stopped grinning. He saw with disfavor a boy arise from out of the bushes along the roadside and run forward, clutching at Hamlet's red-fringed bridle-rein. The boy spoke rapidly. Hamlet listened. Hamlet turned toward Hermetrude. They conferred briefly. She gave orders. With the Picts and the Caledonians following Hamlet, he rode eastward, toward the seashore; and behind these troops went Queen Hermetrude at the head of the War Women of Mel. None entered the pass of Botsuane.

Says Edric: "The parricide has been warned.
Hell helps him. Nevertheless, I have bidden death
to a banquet. One must keep faith with death; and
on this day either Hamlet or I must go up into
Valhalla."

Edric withdrew his forces southerly, along the
upper ridges of Botsuane, and he aligned his men
to advantage in the higher fields which bordered
upon the beach of Straithkeld. So did Hamlet find
his road blocked by the Deiri, and there without
any parley a shrewd battle began, in the open, between the Deiri and the Picts. It was a fierce and
obstinate conflict; each man fought less for victory
than for his own life, beside the bright sea waters,
while many perturbed gulls wheeled and squeaked
overhead, and the salty odors of their home gave
way to the smell of blood.

King Edric got the uppermost of the fighting,
because the Picts had to charge uphill, and moreover Edric was a well-seasoned warrior, whereas
this was Hamlet's first battle. The Picts wavered;
and drawing backward, were put into disorder
through having collided with their own provision
wagons and pack horses. Their ranks broke. They
blundered about like so many swarming bees, jostling and incommoding one another, without dis-
cipline.

"I have him," says Edric.

In the while he was speaking, Hermetrude entered the confused battling, and behind her came the War Women of Mel. These ladies were terrible in action; but Hermetrude surpassed them all. In ardor she so far outstripped her attendants that to every intent she charged the Deiri single-handed, and eight of their most hardy fighting-men had fallen before her ashen lance gave way under repeated blows—being shivered into pieces against the strong shield of Earl Athelstane of Cobham,— and in this manner put Hermetrude to the need of drawing Sleep-Giver, in order to strike off the head of Athelstane as she passed him. She brandished her sword above the fighting, and she made sure that Sleep-Giver was in proper fettle by killing two gentlemen of no special distinction, before she went onward uphill to King Edric and his standard-bearer and his picked body-guard.

Edric dismounted as lightly as if he were yet a boy. With a battle-ax he struck dead his own horse, so as to make flight impossible. Such was the proud custom of the Kings of Deira when they faced doom. Now he faced Hermetrude.

Behind Hermetrude came the War Women cutting and hewing down all who opposed them. No kind of armor could withstand the battle fury of these irresistible ladies, for their swords split open the heads of their adversaries from the top to the

teeth. They took no prisoners. They spared nobody. They attacked the Deiri as when wolves as-
sail sheep. Yet not very many of the army of King
Edric, it should be recorded, fled from the War
Women of Mel. The greater part of that army
remained where they had fought, having no fear in
their hearts, nor any life in their bodies.

Thus was the power of Deira demolished at
Straithkeld.

29

OF THE PIETY OF QUEEN HERMETRUDE

WE SPEAK AS TO HOW THE NEWS REACHED HAM-
let that Wiglerus had been captured. Hermetrude
was not with the young King of Jutland at this
time, for, now the fighting was over, the War
Women of Mel were disporting themselves, profit-
ably, in all parts of the battle-field, by mutilating
and robbing the dead. They find thus, by-and-by,
the body of King Edric.

"Strip my unfortunate dear wooer," says
Hermetrude, smiling, as with her very long, sharp-
pointed tongue, she licked at each corner of her
mouth, "so that through his death I may get the
pleasure, which the Norns did not grant me during
his life time, of beholding King Edric made ready
for an amorous battle in the strength of his manhood."

She was obeyed. They flung down, face upward, the hacked lean naked corpse at her feet.

Then the Queen laughed, very sweetly, to observe what the nibbling years had made out of that
obstreperous young red-headed Edric who, in his

prime, had been so famous for the contentment
and the jealousy which he roused among noble
ladies. But Magnus the Skald did not laugh. Magnus began, instead, to improvise a dirge about how
Time left in tatters all valor and nobleness and
intrepid desires; and he spoke likewise as to how
the grim rage of Time made pale every nature of
beauty, and silenced every kind of applause, and
left hope dead.

"Even so," said Magnus, "has Time dealt with
Edric of Deira: for but a little while ago this Edric
was notable as a lord of spears and as a diminisher
of peace wherever he came; when he went out to
fight, the wolf and the raven followed him, well
knowing that he would provide for them food. He
had great strength and no fear; he was amorous
and very liberal; among the other kings of Britain
he seemed as a green leek grown high among
grasses, or as a gold coin among silver coins. But
now he is carrion; and now, with his own body,
proud Edric of Deira affords to-day his last meal
to the wolf and the raven."

"It will not surfeit them, with any too fat
over-feeding," the Queen of Pictland replied in
good-natured contempt; "nor, for the rest, do I at
all envy the wives of Edric."

"Truly," says Hamlet—who had come for-
ward smilingly, to observe the diversions of his new

wife,—"I think that in place of this skinny wreckage you got in me a far better bargain."

"I agree with you, my dear lord," returned Hermetrude, "even though it is for a reason so small and sapless that a modest gentlewoman would hardly care to raise it in public."

Having thus gently reproved her husband's tendency toward coarseness, she drew her dagger, and she disposed of the body of King Edric after the custom of the Picts. To Freia, who presided over love-affairs, the Queen devoted the proper organs; and besides these, Hermetrude removed the heart, the lungs, and the liver. The lungs and the liver she burned as an offering to the Disir, or guardian spirits, of Hamlet and Hermetrude. But the heart of Edric she cut into four pieces; and these red gobbets she very gracefully cast north and south and east and west, as a sacrifice to Odin the Bestower of Victories, the Wise Wanderer, the Subtle One.

Said Hamlet: "That is a quaint custom; yet it is a niggardly custom. Why should Odin value the fragments of a chopped-up dead man? It is in a living sacrifice that Odin gets pleasure. The fact occurs to me, now we are talking about holy matters, that our men took a few prisoners."

"Then you must let me have them," says Hermetrude, "and you must let me have them at once.

Well-brought-up persons ought always to acknowl-
edge the kindness of Heaven promptly."

With a slow smile of approval, Hamlet delivered up to her the eleven surviving captives, praising her high principles. The happy War Women
of Mel, with a subdued murmur of pious ejacula-
tions, went away from the sandy battle-field to the
uplands of Straithkeld, where they could build, as
was now needed, a broad mound of fresh earth
mould mixed with as many silver coins as proved
available. Upon this mound they fastened all the
screaming prisoners face downward.

While the devout ladies sang reverently in
Odin's honor, Queen Hermetrude removed her
gold-figured corselet, and she turned back the
sleeves of her kirtle. They bring to her a very holy
rock, white in color and inscribed with runes, and
upon this stone she whetted a knife, of the kind
which the Picts called ryting. Afterward Queen
Hermetrude performed the intricate and impres-
sive sacrifice of the blood eagle.

"Now then," says Hamlet, when he saw that
his dear love was handsomely engrossed by her deli-
cate devotions over the second prisoner, "do you
bring to me, down yonder by the seaside, Wiglerus.
And do you bring also that boy who warned us
against entering the pass of Botsuane."

30

WHAT HAMLET DECIDED TO DO: HOW HORVENDILE HELPED HIM

IT WAS IN THIS PLACE HAMLET HAD TALKED WITH Orton when Hamlet was going toward Deira as a hunted fugitive. Now Hamlet sat there alone, an all-conquering king; but by-and-by they send down to Hamlet the boy, and they send Wiglerus also.

As Wiglerus came down unarmed, from the flat battle-field to the sloping seashore, a crane started up before him, and flew seaward lumberingly. The bird stayed so close to the smooth sea's surface that you saw its shadow go with it—a light brown, wavering, twinkling shadow, which floated immediately beneath and just not touching the bird. There had been no fighting here, to disturb this crane from her own proper affairs, which no doubt included a nest near by. These sun-drenched hot white sands, in fact, were marked only by one very long, irregularly curving, dark line of tangled sea-grass, as yet green, washed up by the last high tide. The sea appeared not to move at all except where its gleaming languid waters broke lispingly on the sand, in a stealthy series of cream-colored ripplings which ran southward continuously. It was peculiarly quiet in this place. Since the breeze was landward, you could not hear the voices of the Pictish army, just behind you, upon the higher blood-stained fields.

"It is a pleasingly tranquil place," thought Wiglerus, "in which to meet death; and death will teach me—perhaps—not ever again to behave frivolously in a graveyard. Since it was my own folly which made me this lout's captive, I have no grounds for complaint."

He thought also that, like the sea yonder, Hamlet looked sulky and unusually quiet at the instant.

"You are welcome, my uncle," says Hamlet. "I will attend to you by-and-by." But to the boy who upon that morning had preserved Hamlet and Hermetrude, along with the Pictish army, from destruction, and who had brought about the destruction of the army of Deira and the ruin of King Edric, Hamlet said,—

"Why did you warn me, Alftruda?"

At that, Wiglerus cried out; and then he stayed quite silent when he saw this was indeed Alftruda, dressed like a boy, in ragged brown clothing.

She replied, to Hamlet, very sweetly and clearly, with the composure which best adorns a gentlewoman at jarring moments:

"I could not choose, my husband, but to preserve your life at all costs. My father had compelled me to accompany him so that I might behold the reward of your dissolute behavior. For that reason I deserted him last night. I left his camp in such clothing as—I admit frankly—no queen ought to wear in public. I could not hold back through considerations of modesty. It was not possible for me to assist in your being punished as you perhaps deserve to be punished."

"Why not?" said Hamlet. "I have put upon you every affront and injury I could well contrive. Have you not any proper pride, Alftruda, that on top of this you try to entangle me into gratitude?"

She said then: "I did not think about such matters. I knew only that I could but love and cherish you now your child moves in my body."

"So with my aid—or it may be with the aid of some of your robust kinsmen in the stable, up in some hot hayloft," says Hamlet—"you have been got with child! It needed that only."

Alftruda had flushed somewhat; but she stayed calm and benignant.

"I am tempted, my husband, to make no more

account of you than you do of me. I have not
deserted thus to be deserted and insulted. Yet I
must pardon that also, in the present drunkenness
of your senses."

"I am more sane than you," says fretted Hamlet—"by any account."

The resolute and stonily bright patience of
Alftruda put aside his rudeness, with the resigned
gesture of an implacably high-minded woman who,
without any too much optimism, is trying to instil
into the knowledge of her husband a proper sense
of his misbehavior.

"I know very well, my lord," said Alftruda,
in a continuing quiet rapture of forgiveness, "that
the allurements and persuasions of a bold and
shameless harlot are of great force to entice and
charm the actions of young men. You might, I
think, be somewhat more kindly to your wife and
to the mother of your own dear child than to reject
me for this lewd Scotswoman. I cannot say what
you see in her: her mouth is enormous; and her big
hooked nose is not really a nose, but a beak. Yet
I must endeavor to love her now, because you love
her, and because your will is my will, and because
your happiness is my only contentment."

"There spoke an angel," declared Wiglerus
with conviction.

Hamlet scowled at him, saying: "I do not like these unrestrained pieties. I dislike such frozen perfection."

"You are not worthy of her," says Wiglerus hotly.

"I hope not," said Hamlet. "Hermetrude has a fine nose. I will not have her nose forgiven in this smug way. Nor do I want to be forgiven, either, in this smug way. No, Wiglerus: I cannot endure this pious cool plague of self-complacency. I retreat from it terror-stricken. I seek refuge under the fifty-fourth law of the Gulathing. I pronounce a separation between this woman and me now that she hears my voice in the presence of a witness. So then! the law has been complied with; and I am well rid of this mincing preaching mealy-mouthed half-wit."

"The law requires you should have two or more witnesses," said Wiglerus.

He barked this out, raspingly, now that he had seen the bewildered hurt look in the meek sweet face of Alftruda.

Hamlet answered: "I cannot get any other witness here who would not betray her to Hermetrude. You know that, Wiglerus. You know too what would happen then. I cannot have the idiot murdered. She has saved all our lives. It is an obligation I cannot overlook. Hermetrude would over-

look it. That was why I gave her my eleven prisoners to play with while I dealt with the pair of
you."

"So this hulking oaf conceals somewhere an
intelligence, after all!" declared Wiglerus; "for
your pious munificence was truly the Greek gift
of a born diplomat."

"Be silent!" says Hamlet. "I had intended to
kill you, Wiglerus, on account of the improper
advances which you made to Queen Hermetrude.
She has been candid with me concerning them."

"In women," said Wiglerus, "candor is indeed
a jewel. It is like a diamond, which we prize on
account of its rarity."

"Be silent!" said Hamlet. "But I shall now use
you to a better purpose. I cannot permit this half-
wit to be injured, no matter how much I would
enjoy choking her with my own hands. There is
no person among the Pict army whom I can believe to be so feeble-minded as not to sell this
woman to Hermetrude out of hand."

"Rather than let Alftruda go free, in all the
appalling destructiveness of her high moral principles," said Wiglerus, grinning a little—and speaking from a point of view somewhere between anger
and complete sympathy.

Hamlet shouted, "Be silent!" He then added:
"Just so. There is only, Wiglerus, you. So it is you,

my uncle, who must now take away this too holy angel out of my hearing before she has begun again to forgive everybody, and before I have gone mad and bitten her. You can get a ship at Thorsby, to convey you both into Denmark. You had better do this before Hermetrude has made an unpleasant end of you both."

Wiglerus says: "I shall avoid meeting the Queen of Pictland willingly. She has a too impetuous nature. And for the sake of your child, Alftruda, you will go with me."

"Yes; but," Alftruda stated firmly, "her nose is hideous."

"That is hardly the point at issue," Wiglerus said. "The true point, Hamlet, to an increasingly harsh conference, is that when I gave up to you this most unrighteously used lady, you made an oath, saying, 'If ever my faith fails her, then let my head answer for it.' Do you take warning, my nephew, that I shall hold you to your oath."

Hamlet laughed. He struck this little Wiglerus, full in the face, brutally.

"I have told you to be silent. It is your business to run my errands without comment. I am a king, and you are a pot-bellied old vagabond as shabby in person as in repute. Do you take my head when you have the power to get it."

Wiglerus did not move. He smiled, by-and-by, with a bleak urbanity. He said,—

"I have that power."

Now Hamlet addressed the zenith, with a great loud blustering which, to the cold fury of Wiglerus, appeared meant in chief to hide the big-muscled young butcher's embarrassment.

"This jack-pudding," cried Hamlet, "is out of his wits."

"It would be very easy"—Wiglerus told him, speaking quite equably—"for me to go now, leaving here in his ignorance the barbarian who strikes an unarmed prisoner. It would certainly be more sensible. Yet I cannot part with you, Hamlet, without speaking five more words."

Hamlet answered: "Do you speak your five words. You do not often stint yourself to five words."

"In fact," Wiglerus granted—even while he noted that the hand he had meant to wave blandly was moving stiffly before his blurred vision, like a jerked wooden toy,—"in fact, loquacity is by way of being with me a foible. I like words. I enjoy playing with words. You must not grudge me this weakness, now that honor is compelling me—I very much fear—to purchase an eternal silence with the speaking of these five words."

"Speak them," said Hamlet. "If ever you could

make an end of speaking, you Wiglerus, then I might make an end of hating you."

"How very like we are, at this instant," thought Wiglerus, "to a pair of dogs bristling at each other, here in this sunlight! And how foolish a thing is honor!"

He said then, aloud, "I am King of Denmark."

Hamlet grunted at that,—in mere surprise at first. His tense huge hand went to his gilded sword-hilt slowly. Wiglerus noted that as the hand moved, the thick blond hairs on it glinted in the sunlight like silver. Hamlet moistened his lips. But he said only,—

"Explain."

"My father is dead, Hamlet. My two brothers have killed each other in their efforts to get his crown. The crown comes to me. It follows that you have here as your prisoner, and at your disposal, your liege-lord and your eternal enemy. I shall not forgive any part of to-day's work. I shall not remit the oath made to me at Middleburgh. Rest assured of that. It follows you must make an end of me, here and at once, or else before very long I shall destroy you."

Hamlet said: "You might have gone free in silence. You have no right to put this temptation upon me."

Wiglerus shrugged. The unpleasant tenseness

of complete fury had departed from him, as he observed with approval; the palms of his hands were sweating copiously, but in other respects he felt quite at ease in the while that, as if from a distance, he heard his own lazily modulated voice saying:

"I will not cheat. I will not make any fault in honor. So do I assure myself. At bottom, Hamlet, I believe I am moved by selfishness. I would like to save my soul if—as remains always possible—I do indeed possess any such article. I have been guilty of much wastefulness and of considerable folly; but of no absolute wickedness or very great infamy. Even though I have not won for my head any halo, I have nevertheless managed to keep my hands tolerably clean. If I leave this beach alive I cannot do that any longer."

He spoke simply, almost pleadingly.

"You see, Hamlet, I shall have to use war and treachery and much ruthlessness in order to destroy you. I shall have to traffick in many sorts of infamy. And I shall do it. Stay certain of that. But I shall not like having to do these things."

Said Hamlet: "I pity both of us. Honor is a hard master. I could save all the north parts of the world much trouble by striking off your head here and now. But for me to do that would be unworthy of Horvendile's son."

Looking pensively at the son of Fengon, Wiglerus answered,—

"Very certainly, that is one aspect of the matter."

Then Hamlet said: "It was here, upon this same beach of Straithkeld, that I profited by the advice of gray cunning. It got me great eminence. I profit now by the advice of honor. I must do what befits the son of brave Horvendile. If ruin comes of it, I accept ruin. This woman has preserved me. I can protect her only by liberating my decreed enemy. Go, Wiglerus! The way to your throne is cleared."

"That," Wiglerus replied, in frank disapproval, "is a most absurd gesture. And now"—he went on speaking—"now, I suppose, civility requires it of me to rejoice, with a large deal of fine rhetoric, over getting both my life and a worthy enemy. But I do not rejoice. For one matter, I have not any money for our ship passage. At Vagar, I must tell you, I met with a distressed gentlewoman whose aged and infirm husband was in a most pitiable physical condition; and in my unpractical way, I bestowed upon her every penny which I had with me."

Hamlet said: "I will supply what is needed. But for you to be giving away all your money, out of pure charity, was very nobly done, my uncle."

"No, my nephew," said Wiglerus; "I do not really deserve any praise for that donation, inasmuch as I gave it without thinking about the affair either one way or the other. My action was almost involuntary."

"I do not love you," Hamlet continued, in his heavy self-evident envy of a modesty so heroic. "Your ways are not my ways; and in one way or another way, accident has made enemies of us, from the first. Perhaps the Norns divert themselves, with us two for playthings. Yet in all your dealings— my decreed enemy,—I have found you to be a gallant and great-hearted gentleman. So, do you mark this," said Hamlet, fidgeting, and speaking still more harshly, in the young man's discomfort— "mark that if you were indeed but a private gentleman, I would now be apologizing for the blow which I gave you in anger."

"But honor," said Wiglerus, appreciatingly, "honor does not permit a king to apologize to another king. A dissension between kings has to be wiped out, at a fair remove from their persons, with the blood of their subjects. Yes, I quite follow you, King of Jutland. Destruction and rapine and death and perfidy alone can make an honorable peace between us. Meanwhile, my dear boy, let us embrace."

They did so; and Wiglerus kissed Hamlet upon each cheek.

"You must pardon my display of emotion now that we pledge ourselves to this mutual homicide," remarked the King of Denmark, grinning slightly. "It springs from remorse. I should not have stopped to talk with Earl Sigmund's wife. But I did waste time in that fashion. In consequence, Horvendile was killed; and out of his death has come disaster after disaster, inevitably. Well! but yet larger troubles must follow now—my good cousin of Jutland,—until at our battlings' end the one of us two kings has killed the other."

Then Wiglerus looked about him, a bit sadly, so that he might always remember the hot bright salty-smelling place, and the broad opal-tinted waters breaking against the sand in very long cream-colored ripplings which ran southward. He had thought to die in this special place; he knew now it was upon this beach he was leaving all that remained to him of youth.

31

OF WIGLERUS IN THE EAST: THE BATTLES IN JUTLAND

"UNTIL ONE OF US TWO KINGS HAS KILLED THE other," said Wiglerus, yet again—after his coronation and the fatal ending, at Hundorp, of his trouble with Thorfin's wife,—"there cannot be any quiet in Denmark. I prefer quiet."

It is related how a herald came out of Elsinore, toward Jutland, and into the royal palace at Sundby; and how this herald said to King Hamlet, with a suitable mixing of high-mindedness and of regret and of reproof and of politeness:

"My lord Wiglerus, ever to be feared, the unconquered King of the Danes, is entering into this province to take back his own. If you surrender to him all Jutland, meekly and utterly, it is permitted you to depart out of his kingdom unhurt. You must take with you that lewd woman who has stolen the place of your lawful wife. The King of the Danes cannot condone any such moral turpitude. If you resist my lord Wiglerus, you shall be counted unworthy of continued living."

Hamlet would have answered these demands formally; but Hermetrude, in the first flush of that noble lady's indignation, was too quick for him. She spoke fluently; and by the more poignant passages of an extemporary address, concerning the private life of Alftruda and the personal traits of King Wiglerus, she evoked from the attendant earls of Jutland an unwilling tribute of surprise. These hardy pirates had found out, with astonishment, they were still able to blush. Hermetrude then cut off both the ears of the herald, as a symbol of the deafness with which she had heard his message; she caused human excrement to be thrust into the mouth which had uttered his message, so as to indicate her reply to it; and in this way she dismissed him with a double reward, of insult and of mutilation, to show for his trouble.

Wiglerus then led into Jutland a chosen company of broad-shouldered and brave young cutthroats. They brought with them (the story says) green pennons and banners of various forms glitteringly emblazoned with the red dragon of the Harfaagers; they carried lances with gleaming points; they wore shining helmets and coats of mail. They rode proudly, in many-colored garments, mounted upon stallions which champed at foaming bits. They advanced in a befitting splendor, and they came with heroic joy, to butcher their opponents in accord with the time-approved traditions of chivalry. They were an army well regulated in the camp, and upon the battle-field they were terrible to the foe.

But Hamlet, upon the advice of Hermetrude, did not meet them on any battle-field. Instead, very much as Edric had done at Botsuane, now Hamlet laid an ambuscade just north of Voer; and the invaders rode into it without hesitation. They came thus to the Vorsaa, and found the stone bridge had been destroyed before them. Behind them, upon both sides, the concealed forces of Jutland closed in. Hamlet shattered that fine company. He dispersed the superb army of Wiglerus as a housewife sweeps away dust.

"I have underestimated this young man, who has the supreme good sense not to imitate me by fighting an open and honorable battle," said Wiglerus, ruefully, as he escaped with some half-dozen followers. He got safe to Elsinore, and he there reconstructed his notions of modern warfare.

He had renewed reason to do this, after Hermetrude took the field. She crossed the Limfjord, and rapine, burning and slaughter went with her, now that the Jutlanders under her leadership made spoil of the country and put the subjects of Wiglerus to the sword. She laid siege to Aalborg, and on the eleventh day of the siege a part of the town

was set on fire, and then the Danes who inhabited
Aalborg surrendered to Hermetrude injudiciously.
Of these Danes some were hanged, some were cast
living into the flames of their former homes, and
some were hacked into pieces with battle-axes; the
leading gentlemen of the neighborhood were
thrown headlong from the walls of Aalborg, and in
the market-place nine members of the town council were displayed hung upside down upon iron
hooks fastened through their genitals. The children
of Aalborg were tossed about merrily upon the
points of the Jutlanders' lances, while the screaming mothers of these children were being quieted
with such haste that the less handsome of them
were not even raped before having their throats
slit.

"My niece is more thorough-going than Hamlet," remarked Wiglerus, pallid with disgust. "Because of the innate good taste of womankind, she
does not trim the butcher's apron of war with the
spangles of chivalry. And she is wholly right; for
I now see the combination is inharmonious. Let us
prove to Queen Hermetrude that a reformed romanticist can be as bone-bare of chivalry as any
woman breathing."

This much Wiglerus did. He brought the entire Danish fleet to Karendal; he destroyed, with
some haste but with complete efficiency, the small

navy of Jutland; and he made a station at Karendal for his ships. In charge of these vessels he left
a sufficient garrison after Wiglerus had landed his
army. He then advanced in such overwhelming
strength that Hermetrude of necessity retreated
toward Emb, to join forces with Hamlet. So for
the second time did Wiglerus the King come into
Jutland, and he came now without any old-fashioned display of royal pomp or of out-of-date
clemency.

He ordered his Danes to kill the Jutlanders,
men, women and children alike, but always, when
this was possible, to hang or to strangle them, so
that none might hope to enter Valhalla. He for-
bade any dalliance with living women, permitting
his soldiers to violate only the dead bodies of the
women of Jutland. He instructed his army to burn
each town just as Hermetrude had burned Aalborg;
to plough the tilled fields with salt; to cut down
the woods and the fruit-trees. His passing left the
land bare. His oppressions terrified all Jutland.
There was no resisting the malignity of time-tu-
tored Wiglerus, now that he went about leaving
in every place destruction. Behind Wiglerus, no
windmill turned nor did any chimney smoke; wherever he had been, the cocks ceased their crowing,
and the dogs their barking, so complete was the
ruin behind Wiglerus. Grass grew in what remained

of the houses; briars and white-flowering thorns alone showed where villages had once stood.

The Jutlanders were defeated at Lökken, and yet again at Horne. At Jerslev, the greater part of their army ran away, and disbanded. The loss of their fleet at Karendal hampered them most desperately. It left all their sea-coast at the mercy of Wiglerus, who had not any mercy; it made any escaping from Wiglerus almost impossible. The Jutlanders began to desert Hamlet; many earls quitted him, and the more willingly for that he had destroyed their kinsmen at Sundby; every such apostate was received with bland courtesy by the King of Denmark, without any apparent remembrance of past conflicts, either of opinion or of person. He gave them audience in Hamlet's own royal castle, at Sundby, which Hamlet had now lost along with all his other possessions.

Before the repeated and implacable scowls of fortune, Hamlet gave way. He withdrew into the swamps of Vildmose. His position there was impregnable, forasmuch as no army could advance upon the narrow footpaths which led windingly among the bogs and quicksands of Vildmose. Nor did his few remaining adherents lack for shelter, among plentiful timber, or for food either, where fish and water-fowl and the red deer could be had for the taking. To the other side, Hamlet could not get out of Jutland, or even out of this swamp, which the forces of Wiglerus now surrounded completely.

So the matter rested; and Hermetrude was not pleased by these doings.

32

HOW MAGNUS TROUBLED QUEEN HERMETRUDE IN A SWAMP

"When you and I were at home in Alcluid," says Hermetrude, to Magnus the Skald, "we were in a better place than Vildmose."

"Very truly," replied Magnus; "for that dear home at Alcluid had walls of white bronze and turrets of red bronze. The door posts of that house were colored with purple; the lintel of each door was molded out of fine silver, which Ardan took away in battle from the people of Caledonia. One did not trudge through much evil-smelling mud in order to get into Alcluid. Alcluid was a pleasant home, that was filled with smiling persons; and Hermetrude had command over them all. In the sunny house of Alcluid were silken coverings and red gold and bright drinking-horns. Every third day the pert serving boys spread out new rushes upon its floors. The plump butlers of Alcluid did not attend upon gloom and spitefulness and bad fortune as the guests of Hermetrude at her banquets. In the tiring room of Alcluid were a queen's rings and her bracelets and her crowns and her brooches, and her clothing of blue and green and crimson and her speckled saffron over-robes. Upon the walls of the queen's parlor were hangings of white linen. Alcluid was not an ugly hut, like this hut, with its roof half broken in."

Now all the while he was speaking, the Queen had sat motionless, looking into the hearthfire which alone made this hut habitable. In her large brown eyes the firelight reflected its stir as a shifting and a superficial glittering, so that for the time her eyes seemed to have no depth to them. She moved now, though but as slightly as when a sleeping person wakes of his own accord.

"And yet true love," declared Hermetrude reflectively, "can find contentment under a broken roof, and among the fogs of Vildmose, or in any other place."

"She that owned Alcluid and the things that were in that house," said Magnus, "did not waste her love upon a hunted outlaw among mud-puddles. She was not laughed at, as a short-seeing strumpet. She was beautiful and powerful beyond all the women of this world by the length of a spear cast; and this Hermetrude was loved by every noble person that saw her."

"Yes; that is true," the Queen admitted fair-mindedly; "and the misguided people of Jutland do not love me. They say I am not indeed the wife of Hamlet but only his mistress, because Alftruda is still his wife. So they whisper in secret about me."

"Everywhere," said Magnus, "they spit out their lewdness against you, do these surly snakes. And like scourged curs the Danes yelp at you because you took the town of Aalborg with blood-drenched hands. You live in a never-lifting mist of hatred. Many angers show their teeth at Queen Hermetrude."

"In fact, Magnus, I have found no good fortune, and no happiness either, in this harsh northern land, where the skies are gray and sullen, and the hearts of all persons about me are gray and sullen."

"So by-and-by," returned Magnus, "will be the heart of King Hamlet. The man loves you as yet. But you have been his bright ruin; your fine red lips have nibbled away his strength and his famousness; you have left him bare. He knows that now; and by-and-by he will be asking himself—as you have already asked yourself, Queen Hermetrude,—Was love worth its purchase price?"

"Our love was great. Our love was very heroic," the Queen said unsteadily. "Time and chance shall not ever prevail against our love."

In the firelight you saw the teeth of Magnus.

"Stop smiling," said Hermetrude.

"I smiled only," the dark lean man assured her, "because of the fond joy with which I remember our dear home at Alcluid."

"Indeed, Magnus, but that home was noble; and everywhere it had a name for greatness."

"In the green plains of the open country around Alcluid," said Magnus softly, "were well-tended horses and large flocks of sheep; and herds of swine were in the woods and the valleys; and droves of cattle fed in the tall forests north of Alcluid. Alcluid did not stand in a wet hungry swamp with frogs croaking about its walls in the twilight, or with owls hooting bad prophecies outside its windows in the night time; and at Alcluid there was not a continual fretfulness growing up in any proud woman's heart to become hatred."

Hermetrude answered: "I do not in the least understand you, Magnus. You may go away now."

The Queen's headsman arose, and he bowed with half mocking civility.

"I shall return," he said, "when you have need of me."

33

THE TALKING TOGETHER OF HERME-
TRUDE AND HAMLET IN VILDMOSE

Now it must be told how Queen Hermetrude continued to dislike living in a draughty leaking hut among mud-flats. Far oversea was her well-remembered kingdom, in that Pictland for which, among the discomforts of this gloomy swamp, her heart began to hunger more and yet more patriotically. Her conscience likewise began to trouble her, with high-minded doubts as to whether it were the proper part of a queen thus to abandon her people?

She had left her kingdom in the hands of her sister, Estrild, so that Hermetrude might accompany her husband across the North Sea and, through her superior knowledge of warfare, assist him to retain Jutland. Not to forsake Hamlet in his danger had seemed right to her—at an impulsive moment, when her too generous nature had perhaps yielded to an excess of charity, as she now admitted with contrition. Yet at the time this really had seemed to be her duty, even after the

outrageous imbecility of Hamlet, in allowing Alftruda and Wiglerus to go free when Hamlet had
them both in his power, and a skilled executioner
within reach of Hamlet's voice.

It was a performance upon which Hermetrude
had been compelled to comment, ever since then,
continually, with the frankness it merited; and to-
night she recurred to the horrid theme, just in
passing; for, as she explained to Hamlet, at outset,
this was the very last thing in the world she desired to discuss with anybody, or even so much as
to think about. This was a topic concerning which
she was firmly resolved to speak not a word, either
one way or the other. She asked merely, of a nau-
seated universe, whether the insanity or the wickedness of Hamlet's conduct at Straithkeld would
figure—in the unprejudiced eyes of a right-minded
person—as the more repulsive? She described, simply for his own good, the one sort of moonstruck
criminal who would ever have committed any
such action. And in mere justice to herself, she followed up her résumé of Hamlet's deficiencies in
general with a statement of her own undeserved
affliction in particular.

"You have placed me in a peculiarly embarrassing situation, Hamlet, as you must permit me
to tell you for the sake of everybody concerned.
By the approved law of every civilized Nordic

kingdom, if you wished to divorce that Alftruda of
yours, you had, as you knew perfectly well, to pronounce your divorce where she could hear your
voice in the presence of witnesses."

"Yes; but, my dear—"

"There was present only one witness, in Wiglerus. Wiglerus has been accused of a great many
things, including duplicity, but never, I believe, of
being plural."

"None the less, my pet—"

"So the slut sticks to it that she is still your
wife; the law seems to bear her out; and your subjects make bold to question my respectability. Now
where does that leave me?"

"It leaves you in my heart, my dearest, en-
throned there forever—"

"That is all very well, Hamlet; but pawing
at me, with your big sweaty hands, does not answer
my question. Nor do I think it is mere morbid curiosity, when a woman wishes to find out whether
or not she is married to the man she is living with.
It is a question in which any rational woman would
be interested."

"You alone, Hermetrude, are my wife, in the
eyes of Heaven—"

"I am not talking about Heaven. I am talking
about Jutland. There is a distinct difference. If
only you had shown the consideration, and the

mere decent respect which every king owes to the law, to summon any one of my soldiers to be another witness, there would have been no trouble whatever."

"But then, my dear, that soldier would have betrayed Alftruda to you—"

"He would have done nothing of the sort. He would have notified me of the wicked whining creature's whereabouts, because the soldiers of Pictland are loyal to their sovereign; and that, you must let me tell you, is a deal more than can be said for the soldiers of Jutland, who have left us here in this cold swamp—"

"—Then you would promptly have murdered Alftruda—"

"Never in my whole life, Hamlet, have I heard of such nonsense! Murder is an absurd word. Murder has nothing whatever to do with it. I would merely have considered it my moral duty to see to it that the righteous demands of justice were attended to, after the woman's outrageous conduct with Wiglerus—"

"Hermetrude, you do not know anything about her conduct with Wiglerus—"

"Do I not indeed, when I know perfectly well how that lewd Wiglerus behaves the very instant he is left alone with a young woman?"

"Oh! ah!" says Hamlet. "What do you mean by that?"

She replied with benign dignity: "I mean only that I have my womanly intuitions. Men do not understand such matters. So let us not discuss them. Wiglerus is a most horrible libertine, I can assure you. And when I remember that you had him as your prisoner! and that you then let him go free, in order that he might take your kingdom away from you! and imprison both of us here in this dreadful swamp—!"

Hamlet said wearily: "We get nowhere by arguing the matter. A thing done has an end; and this thing was done honorably. Alftruda had saved your life and my life and all our lives. She had brought about the death of her own father on account of her unmerited love for me—"

"Since when, will you please tell me, Hamlet, did parricide become a wholly praiseworthy action?"

He answered, deeply shocked: "But you twist my words, Hermetrude, into an unfair and infamous meaning. A parricide is one who kills his father with his own hands; and for a parricide there can be no forgiveness. Most certainly, I would not ever condone parricide, in any possible circumstances. To the contrary, as becomes a good Viking, I entreat of Heaven that such sin may be punished eternally, both in this world and in the next world."

"Oh, very well then!" said Hermetrude with impatience. "I cry amen."

"And besides that, Hermetrude, the point here is that honor had put upon me a plain obligation to save Alftruda in the one way which was open. So I did this. I had not any choice, my dear, except to keep clean my honor."

Hermetrude said only, with the condensed ardor of uxorial frankness,—

"Your honor!"

Hamlet spoke then in a meditative, rather low voice which startled her; for he had begun to speak easily and equably, and yet half as though he spoke in a dream. She sat stiffly erect; her hand went to her partly open lips. This man she perceived to be fey (as the Norse called it) under the dark rapture of doom; and his talking was not any longer the blunt abrupt speech of Hamlet's daily usage.

Hamlet said: "It was not easy to do that which I did upon the beach of Straithkeld; for until then I had prospered unbelievably. I had revenged honorably the death of my loved father, achieving justice against incredible odds; and the affair had won for me a great name. I had got my kingdom; I had got wealth and comfort; and in you, dear Hermetrude, I had got likewise the one woman whom my heart has worshipped utterly and whom my heart

must now serve forever until death has made cold
my heart. It was not easy, and it was perhaps not
wise, to risk so many fine things; yet my honor
commanded me to risk them all, rather than to destroy that meek and great-hearted and pure-
minded and wholly detestable idiot to whom both
you and I, Hermetrude, owed even our lives. So
I did risk these things, of necessity; and now I have
lost them. What is most bitter of all, is that I have
lost likewise your love. Yet the son of brave Horvendile could not have acted differently. Were the
choice offered me yet again, now that my luck has
turned against me, and my life is near its end, I
would not alter my choice in order to have back
these possessions, not even your lost faith in me,
not even your denied tenderness, O my dearest.
For all comfort passes, and all sweets turn sour, and
each one of us must come at long last to his ugly
death; but there is that in us which will outlive
life, I believe, and we ought not to soil it for all
the luxuries that are in this world. So there is no
more to be said."

Hermetrude replied, with a tinge of sullen-
ness, but with complete common-sense,—

"There is this much to be said at least, Hamlet,
—that without consulting my wishes, you have
dragged me into this swamp, because of these insane notions about honor."

"Honor is not merely a notion," he returned. "It is not a thing written about idly in old legends. It is a commandment written very plainly in the heart of each man that lives, if only he be brave enough to read it. Through cowardice he may come to ignore that writing, and indeed, with the aid of continued ignoring, he may come by-and-by to erase it utterly. But when that happens, Hermetrude, the man is dead; and though his body may go on breathing, it is but the body of an animal— oh, a quite harmless and good-natured animal, perhaps,—which continues to eat and to breed and to sleep, not discontentedly. But I will not die slowly in this manner. I will not die tangled up in bedcovers, like cowardly Fengon. I will die with my manhood full upon me, as befits my brave father's son."

Such was the speaking of Hamlet when he had become fey; and Hermetrude considered it toplofty enough to figure with large credit in a public address, but unpractical as a method of getting you out of a swamp.

Yet so considerate of all male imbecility is the condoning common-sense of womankind that Hermetrude did not at this time make any further attempt to restore this haggard madman to his senses in general, or even to induce a more proper sense of his obligations toward her. She remembered, none the less, the past. She remembered that, at Alcluid, when this man first took advantage of her innocence, he had sworn to her an eternal fidelity. Yet here, already, her fine-talking fond lover of yesterday was considering the comfort of no less than two other people, when the continued existence of either one of them had conflicted with the known wishes of Hermetrude.

It was humiliating (her thoughts went on) to see how very lightly her own husband appraised her desires, when all that mere common-sense required of him was the beheading of two persons. If only he had dealt with her frankly, after the fighting at Straithkeld, then everything would have passed in smoothness. Magnus would have attended to old Wiglerus, and to his damned Alftruda too, without involving Hamlet and Hamlet's insane masculine honor one way or the other. But instead, Hamlet had meanly taken advantage of his confiding wife's most high and holy instincts, by packing her off to divine worship, while the tall idiot contrived the escape of her most annoying enemies and his own destruction. Hamlet had thus entrapped her, through his moonstruck notions about honor, into this damp dreadful swamp, from which there was no getting out.

—Except at a price, Hermetrude reflected.

She sighed then. When she next spoke, it was

[218]

about the true love which existed between Hamlet and herself, in spite of, as Hermetrude was convinced, an occasional difference of opinion such as no married couple, in the nature of things, could always avoid. She spoke gently and very nobly; and Hamlet replied with grave tenderness, quietly, in a sort of half-humble gratitude.

Afterward Hermetrude summoned Magnus the Skald, and in private she gave him his instructions.

34

VISIT OF MAGNUS TO WIGLERUS

WE TAKE UP THE STORY AND RELATE MORE ABOUT Wiglerus. The King of Denmark was seated, upon a bench, behind an oaken desk, which was so long and narrow in its shape as less to resemble a desk than a counter. Upon the surface of this desk you saw a Latin manuscript of the King's best loved poet, Quintus Horatius Flaccus, and the tiny faintly tinted figure of a draped woman dancing, and a human skull with its top sawed off, and a blue-and-yellow majolica pot which contained small red roses.

Just back of Wiglerus hung a Byzantine painting of three very stiff and haggard-looking young persons of indeterminate sex, each one of whom wore fastened at the rear of the head a brightly gilded disk. And Magnus the Skald, in an arm-chair of carved oak, sat facing the reflective King of Denmark,—who at this special instant was twirling about a crimson pen, between his fore-finger and his middle-finger, consideringly.

"Her terms are somewhat surprising," said

Wiglerus by-and-by, "in view of the past,—or at any rate, of the more recent past. Mere rationality perishes, however, before a lady so direct, so enterprising, and so beautiful. I agree to the terms of Queen Hermetrude. You may take back that message."

"I shall do so, Majesty," replied Magnus.

"—Whereafter," said Wiglerus, "it is my desire you shall enter my service. I shall have need of you."

"And I trust, Majesty, to serve both of you long and faithfully."

"To serve both of us, Magnus, may not be permitted you when once this affair is concluded."

The skald looked at Wiglerus for some while; and the face of Magnus changed.

"You, Majesty," he remarked, "are a king after my own heart. I foresee that under your patronage my art will flourish."

"And you shall be repaid," Wiglerus promised; but Magnus waved that aside, indulgently.

"The artist," he protested, "does not labor for money. A living wage is, of course, to be desired; but above all, the true artist must have a free field in which to employ his talents unhampered. You will grant me that field; and in return for a not exorbitant fee, I can promise you, over and above my entire faith, an occasional masterpiece."

"What fee do you require, Magnus?"

"The patriotic privilege, my lord King, now and then to rid you of inconvenient adversaries."

"Do you mean, Magnus,"—and Wiglerus looked doubtful—"that I should permit you to kill off any and all public enemies for your private amusement?"

But to the skald that seemed a too sweeping way to phrase the matter.

"I mean, rather, that among the conventionalities of our perhaps over-refined civilization, it is my endeavor to revive the natural language of the human heart in dealing with the most profitable of all poetic themes.—Which is, of course, death."

"On the contrary, the most lofty, and indeed the one pure, form of poetry," returned Wiglerus, "is what the inefficiencies of our language-makers restrict me to term 'being in love.' "

And the King spoke with animation; for he faced heresy. Here was a blaspheming of the philosophy which had guided Wiglerus, that cool-hearted hedonist, throughout life. Wiglerus leaned forward, putting down the crimson pen upon the desk before him; he smiled reminiscently; and he continued:

"—For I too was once a poet, my over-bloodthirsty Magnus, before I dwindled down into versemaking and thence to mere kingship; and I thus found that being in love is the most splendid of stimulants. It heightens the faculties; it fertilizes the mind; and it makes living, quite indescribably, more intense. One observes an anemone or a full moon, for example, which remains forever unforgettable, long after the current moons and anemones of a dozen years have passed disregarded. Yet it was not really a superior moon or a more delicately colored anemone: it happened, such was its good luck, to be seen with the peculiarly intensified vision of a lover. And so is it with every one of the other senses; but in particular, I believe, with the sense of touch, forasmuch as in the finger-tips and in the tactile nerves in general of the lover, alone of trousered humankind, may be enkindled an insane and forever remembered rapture."

—As when this or the other happened, Wiglerus went on to explain, in the while that he expatiated, with extreme grace and vividness, out of no incompetent knowledge.

The retired amorist spoke, as always, with discretion; yet his theme led him, of necessity, into a luxuriance of the explicit which, in this place, it appears well to omit; and he ended his catalogue by remarking,—

"For a man lives to the full only when he is under the influence of being in love."

"He dies to the full in any event," Magnus returned bleakly; "and what does his life amount to then? It affords at utmost the subject for a dirge."

"The fatal drawback to being in love," Wiglerus resumed—stroking pensively the skull of Gissur Syr, which he treasured nowadays as a desk ornament,—"is that the young woman involved is too impetuous. She insists, always, upon ending this superb ecstasy with an indecent haste, either by electing more or less permanently, under the license of marriage, to sleep with somebody else— which to the self-respecting poet cannot but proclaim her to be an idiot,—or else by going to bed with the poet himself, who is thus forced to discover the recipient of his semen to be nothing very unusual after all. If in this matter of selecting their bedfellows young women could but acquire complete indecision and backwardness as a lifelong habit, then would every poet remain eternally faithful and forever enraptured by his unsatiated hopefulness. Poetry would then flourish everywhere; to the other side, now that I think of it, the human race would perish, and the poet would have no audience."

"So that here again," said Magnus, "we confront death, which is the fixed end of all action and of all theorizing."

The King did not answer at once. Instead, he fingered the small figure of the dancing woman, and he moved it to the right, with extreme care, by about four inches. It had become, nowadays, a nervous habit with King Wiglerus thus to move or to straighten some portable object whenever he fell into thought.

"I am not saying," Wiglerus continued, "that out of being in love a poet will always, or even often, get a fine poem written down upon parchment. I mean, rather, that all written poetry is minor poetry. It at best is but an adulterated and very thin version of that poetry which poets alone know about, and can know about only while they are under the influence of being in love. For soundness, for variety, and for gusto, there is no other poetry which equals being in love. For anybody to descend from that pure quintessence of poetry to clerical labor is a degradation. It is a betrayal of his splendid past; it is an abominable action such as no person of honor would commit. In this manner do I infer that a responsible and conscientious poet will not ever prostitute his art by writing verses."

He spoke reasonably; but dark Magnus (he decided) had listened to him with the fretted mulishness of any other artist whose notions are not being humored, completely, by everybody within earshot.

"The poetry which is begotten by love," declared Magnus restively, "remains always lyrical. It is poignant perhaps; in any case, it is brief. For that reason I prefer the epic compositions of death, which last forever. I do not criticize the methods of other poets; I grant freely that your own method, by which no poet would ever write anything, would in the long run improve all literatures; and I say merely it is death alone which inspires Magnus."

"Yet love is vivacious, Magnus; and death is dull."

"Why, but assuredly, my lord King, death is dull; and is it not the mark of every right-minded person to prefer, in all forms of art, dulness? Why do you interpose such frivolous objections?" cried Magnus, thrusting out an enraged forefinger.

"I withdraw them meekly, my good Magnus," said Wiglerus, smiling at the man's zeal; "for indeed I do not know of any sound judge of art who does not admire dulness resoundingly."

"And that, King Wiglerus, you must let me tell you, that is quite as it should be, in the great democracy of art. The dull-minded, here as everywhere else upon earth, compose the majority. It is but fair they should have the casting vote in the selection of their leaders and in the award of all prizes."

Wiglerus shrugged; and the skald went on

speaking, in tones which henceforward were less liberally flavored with the indignation of an earnest-
minded person addressing a fribbler.

"But as I was saying, it is death alone which
inspires Magnus. I say also that when I seek inspiration, I have found it better to compose with
my eye upon the object; and that I prefer, without stooping to any wicked and dishonest plagia-
rism, to evolve my own theme."

"In the form of a corpse," said Wiglerus. "Yes;
I can find no flaw in your logic; and in brief, you,
as an elegist, are compelled to pursue murder for
art's sake."

"I lament the necessity," replied Magnus; "yet
the sincere artist, who gives over his life to his art,
cannot well grudge it the life of some other person. So .must I provoke constantly the remunera-
tive spectacle of death, because to regard it inspires
me with a rich ecstasy of terror; and it thus en-
ables me to pour forth my panic anguish in the
form of a broken-hearted dirge or a fine elegy. It
follows that very often, my lord King, has my
keening been uplifted, in moving accents of deso-
lation and horror, beside the pathetic aloof dead,
to bewail one or another client who, with such
skill as I have mastered through long and patient
practice, has been cut off, it may be, in the prime
of his youth, or it may be in the staunch pride and

perfection of full manhood; or upon still other occasions, in an honor-laden old age."

"Yet, Magnus,"—and Wiglerus cleared his
throat—"you do not mention infancy. Would your
sanguinary muse not find the death of a child—
even of a rather small child—to be acceptably
spirit-stirring?"

Magnus showed his very white and sharp looking teeth in a smile, which partook of the lascivious,
during the instant before he moistened his lips; and
answered:

"It is a handsome theme, which has always
shocked me superbly. Over the unfinished career
and the unfulfilled promise of resplendent youth
my imagination has soared perhaps to its highest;
and in soaring has struck unforgettably its most
haunting note of pathos. That question"—Magnus
added with diffidence—"I may not presume to de-
cide. It is needful that every great artist should
leave to posterity the selection of his masterworks."

The King looked at him intently; and the insane blood-lust of this furtive creature, Wiglerus
thought, was quite horrible; even so, you could get
profit out of it, by using tact.

"Very well, then," says Wiglerus. "I have need
of you, Magnus; and posterity is wholly welcome
to any good which it may incur, hereafter, through
your induced inspirations. We agree merely that I

am to reap the first crop, here in Jutland. With that settled, do you now take back my message to Queen Hermetrude, while I go to Alftruda and to that thriving brat whom Hamlet begot on her body."

"Ah, yes," replied Magnus, comprehendingly. He licked his lips yet again.

35

THE WOMEN AT THORË: WHAT GERUTH PAID FOR HER WICKEDNESS

TRIUMPHANT WIGLERUS HAD LODGED ALFTRUDA in the guest house, not of the King of Denmark, but of the King of Jutland, at Thorë; and there her son had been born, to Geruth's contentment. Here at last—as a beaming grandmother explained, without failing to season her delight with a proper amount of plaintiveness—was somebody akin to her from whose doings she might hope to derive a moderate amount of pleasure; since the child in all probability would not be squabbling with anybody for years, not even with his most near and intimate relatives.

If only, Geruth continued, men could contrive to show a little common-sense at odd moments, then life would not be made invariably and utterly miserable. But what with your father's strangling your mother and then getting himself strangled—or at any rate smothered in bed, which amounted to the same thing, practically, so far as went the feelings of any properly affectionate

daughter,—and your husbands' being killed time
and again before your very eyes, and your brothers' murdering each other all over the church, and
your only child's going to wrack and ruin, on account of that dreadful creature down yonder in
the swamp, there was simply not any end to the
inconsiderate things which men did, without stopping to think that an intelligent person really
would like to have a moment's peace, if just now
and then. Nobody (the Queen Dowager of Jutland
concluded) could deny that; not many women
would have had the patience, in her place, not to be
fretting over such troubles; and that much she felt
it her plain duty to say, even though, for one, she
did not believe in talking to other people about
your troubles.

Wiglerus agreed with Geruth, cordially; and
he so kept her in a state of vocally plaintive but
complete contentment, by admitting she was the
most miserable and the most continuously ill-
treated of all living beings.

In point of fact, as Wiglerus observed, in
silence and with an ironic sense of amusement, his
sister nowadays enjoyed life far more than she had
ever done hitherto. She had been made, even in the
teeth of her talents for the unintentionally comic,
the pivot of a most horrible tragedy, and the object
of Fengon's heroic but fatal devotion; yet to the

comfort-loving temperament of Geruth no one of the exalted emotions which roared and blustered about her had ever become congenial. She had endured being the heroine of a high-pitched and fiery colored romance without ever accepting, at heart, her dire rôle as being anything but a nuisance. And if in addition she had sinned unforgivably, from the standpoint of any sound moralist, yet almost all her iniquity had been prompted by simple good temper and by a kindly desire not to hurt Fengon's feelings.

Nowadays, as an unmarried king's only surviving sister, she presided over the court of Denmark with amiability and even with a fluttered touch of the dignified. She was free to indulge her genuine kindliness toward everybody with whom she came in contact. She did not actually worry about her son Hamlet, except in social converse, as a polite matter of form (so Wiglerus decided), because the imagination of Geruth did not really grasp the existence of any person whom she did not see and talk with at least once a week.

She, for the rest, was under no compulsion to take part in illicit heroisms. She, above all, at this halcyon period of a respite from high-minded iniquity, had the time to get out into the kitchen and to cook for Wiglerus, with her own plump capable hands, what she described as something fit to eat.

Her childlike enjoyment of the zest with which he
—or for that matter, anybody else—could not but
partake of the results, Wiglerus found to be pathetic, somehow, after you had once compared his
sister's wide flushed smile with her flaming name for
great turpitude.

Geruth, he decided, was a born and indeed a
supremely gifted cook, out of whom destiny, without any least success, had attempted to make a
wicked and tragic personage. He wondered if perhaps Clytemnestra, and Jezebel, and Guenevere
also, might not have preferred, at heart, to potter
about in the kitchen, or to attend to their own
sewing in comfort, rather than to strut abroad,
down the great highways of legend, in that full-
blown iniquity which (it remained wholly possible) had been imposed upon each one of these ill-
starred ladies by the incurable romanticism of most
male creatures?

Meanwhile Geruth was talking, at a large remove from any of these philosophic considerings,
about the need of a wellborn, really good nurse for
her grandson. She knew of a widow, it developed,
who might suit. Her husband had been killed at
Aalborg—by that Hermetrude herself, so Geruth
had heard,—and the unfortunate woman had been
injured more or less during the capture of the town,
in addition to matters which nobody could gain

anything by discussing, inasmuch as we all understood what soldiers were like, and always had been,
no doubt. So you could not expect anything else.
At any rate, her step-children had treated her most
abominably afterward, with all sorts of rudeness
and law-suits and bribing the witnesses, so everybody said; and had left her quite penniless. It
showed you how Odin watched over us all, because
in her destitute condition the poor lady would be
more than glad to take whatever was offered her;
and besides that, Geruth, according to the Queen
Dowager's departing statement, did not intend to
put up with any nonsense about eating along with
the family. She meant, instead, to speak plainly.

The King of the Danes was left, in the garden
at Thorë, to face Alftruda and the small son of
Hamlet with an air of some uncertainty.

36

THE CHILD AT THORË: THE COLD INIQUITY OF ALFTRUDA

IT IS TOLD HOW WIGLERUS SAYS, TO ALFTRUDA, "So my young enemy is to be provided with a nurse who will defend and strengthen him to destroy me?"

He reached out his comely well-tended hand toward the child; and the King stroked caressingly the long oval-shaped head of young Eric.

"It seems only last week that he was more like a small boiled ape than a human being," said Wiglerus critically. "And yet, even then, to touch that flesh which is half your flesh—and one-quarter my flesh, Alftruda,—wakened a quiet warm thrill in all my body. I could not help loving the droll ugly helpless animal."

"He was never ugly. He was a particularly fine baby," said Alftruda, bristling.

Wiglerus answered: "As babies go, he was no doubt all that he should be. I do not understand much more about babies than I do about the Providence which imposes any such exorbitant tax upon

the luxury of love-making. I know only that in due
course this small, wiry, listening, alert, half-
suspicious creature, here under my hand, will develop into a self-respecting Nordic gentleman. He
will then almost certainly kill me, if he can manage
it; and I find the reflection of some interest."

"Dear, faithful, noble and quite absurd Wiglerus!" she replied, smiling. "How can you think
about such morbid nonsense? You have been Eric's
protector and the protector of his mother when
they had not any other friends; and my son will
always love you as his foster-father."

The King now regarded her with dark and
slightly narrowed eyes, which had become rather
forlorn looking.

"I am not certain of that, Alftruda; for life
changes us; and there will be upon him, it is possible, the obligation to avenge his true father."

She asked quietly, "Have you killed Hamlet?"

Wiglerus grinned, with thin lips, saying: "I
trust never to kill Hamlet. It would leave me entangled in a blood-feud with his son. This brat here
would then perhaps murder me; and to be murdered I would not like. To the other side, if I acted
rationally, and disposed of your Eric before he had
grown old enough to be dangerous, you would become irritated. I can even infer, from the present
expression of your face, that you quite possibly

would put an end to our friendship. So you see, my dear, I cannot afford to kill Hamlet. Nevertheless, I am bound in honor to square our accounts with him. All that, however"—Wiglerus declared, shrugging,—"is but a dreary part of my need to behave, externally at any rate, like a gentleman. So let us now talk about more pleasant matters such as may suit better this small garden which you make magical. But no, Alftruda! I retract that statement; for you make this unimportant simple garden seem my true home. You see, I peculiarly like holly-hocks; they have a sturdy rusticity such as no other flower possesses. This small regiment of your white and pink holly-hocks, in their dusty green uniforms, I very much prefer to the regiments of the King of Denmark."

"Then by all means," says Alftruda, "let us talk about holly-hocks. The wind damaged them rather badly, night before last; but they are now straightening up again, nicely enough."

Wiglerus raised his hand.

"I babble about holly-hocks," he admitted, "solely because of the insane obstinacy with which my mind runs upon other matters."

"And what matters may they be?" she asked, with a staid innocence which was not wholly convincing.

"Your color assures me very well, Alftruda,

that you can read my mind without difficulty, or any special pleasure. You have, with one sole exception"—remarked Wiglerus, as his thoughts harked back to Earl Sigmund's wife—"the most lovely skin I have ever seen. And so your cheeks blaze, with a most virtuous indignation, now that you suspect a depraved monarch is about to refer, yet again, to his unhallowed passion for a reputable married woman."

She returned with calmness: "Since Hamlet has not ever divorced me properly, I am still Hamlet's wife. I do not pretend I can any longer be fond of him, since he has left me for that quite hideous, hook-nosed, murdering strumpet. Besides, she has a mouth like a cave. I am all grateful to you, Wiglerus; and indeed I love you very much, my old dear friend—"

"But I"—the man interrupted her, half-angrily—"I have no delusions about you nowadays. Time and your priggish narrow-mindedness, between them, have robbed me of all infatuation. You become far too stout, I perceive; you will soon be like a highly complacent small pink-and-white pig. I perceive also—should you pardon continued frankness—that you are rather stupid. Your bland, fixed, cast-iron self-assurance as to just what is right and just what is wrong, for you and for me and for everybody else, in this wholly insane world, irritates me unfailingly. You would reprove Odin, to his own divine face, without at all raising your voice, should the Father of Ages dare to fall short of your expectations. In brief, you enrage me, Alftruda; you disgust all my finer instincts; at many times I detest you beyond any attained field of eloquence. Yet I do not wish to have you changed in any way, neither in your too opulent waist-line nor in your smug imbecility nor in your belligerent primness. I could not live without you, my heart's dearest—"

His voice broke. Wiglerus cleared his throat. He leaned back on his bench; and he said with composure,—

"I could not live in comfort without you, just as you are; that is certain; nor do I mean to make the attempt."

"But as I have told you—and as I have told you I do not know how often," Alftruda answered —"I am ready to become your concubine whenever you ask it. What more can I say?"

Wiglerus groaned at that; and he remarked, with a slow smile which did not have in it very much merriment:

"Here are indeed the passionate wiles of a seductress! I shall not ever understand you, Alftruda. You offer me your body, out of some strange rigid sense of gratitude, as casually as if it were a plate of cold boiled veal. It seems to you the right thing to offer me your body; and so, you propose fornication because of your strict sense of propriety. Yet all the while—I have no least doubt— you believe you are proposing a mortal sin, of which Heaven will note down every item lewdly; and for every item of which, in painstaking accord with a divinely fixed price list, Heaven will extort payment with an implacability unworthy of Hell."

He saw in the placid face of Alftruda an unexplained sort of compassion. Her small cool hand now rested upon the hand of Wiglerus. She caressed his hand half maternally; and Alftruda continued to speak with the unassailable secure decorum of an exceedingly well-bred gentlewoman.

"I loved Hamlet," she said, "in the way that you would have me love you, dear Wiglerus. So I cannot love anybody, not ever any more, in that way. My love for Hamlet has blazed out. There are in my heart no more tall flamings of any kind. My heart has only its warm friendliness for you, O my poor foolish Wiglerus, who, next to my child alone, are the most dear to me of living creatures. And so, no matter what you may desire, my friend, nor whatever may be the cost of it—why, I desire you to have it. That is quite simple, I think."

"And with that," he replied wrily, "one must be content. I decline, however, to accept an illicit bedfellow by whose naïve iniquity any sort of ardor would be frost-nipped. You are like my deplorable dear sister, Alftruda, in that nature did not design either one of you for a life of toplofty misdemeanor; you have been incommoded by the notions of romantic-minded male persons, none the less; and these still involve you. Very well, then! Nothing whatever can be done about it except only that which I have to do to-night."

37

OF THE AWARD IN THE BARGAINING BETWEEN HERMETRUDE AND WIGLERUS

Now that the ambassador from the Frisians had gone away, with the King's promise to help in betraying Bruin Dromund, Wiglerus sat alone, in his privy chamber, at Sundby. This was the room in which Horvendile had met death. Geruth's broad bed had been replaced by a table of white oak; and upon the table was set forth a handsome supper for two persons. Otherwise all stayed unchanged in this room, which was lighted nobly tonight, with many lamps. In the tapestry at the farther end of the apartment the last Nibelungs were still dying heroically.

Here Wiglerus waited. Meanwhile he read, contentedly and with warm appreciation, a romance of the warring which the Greeks made against Troy in the old days; and tears gathered in his eyes, for the King delighted in the tenderness and the nobility of the tale's telling.

They bring in a veiled woman clothed in subdued purple; behind her followed Magnus the Skald. Wiglerus put by his romance, and he arose affably. Then when the guards had gone away, the high King of Denmark said:

"You are welcome, my niece. I must ask your pardon for the apparent incivility of requiring you to come to me; yet it was not possible for me to pay my respects in person so long as you elected to hold your court in the puddles of Vildmose. I am subject to rheumatism. But here, upon dry land and over this supper table, I make bold to hope, we may settle all our family affairs in quiet and cosiness."

Without removing the gray veil which hid her face, Hermetrude spoke abruptly.

"You have made sport with us long enough. I am not a heron or a frog, that I can live penned up in a swamp forever with a ruined madman. What is it you require?"

Wiglerus was explicit. He said,—

"I want the head of Hamlet."

"You shall have that," she replied.

"Come now," says Wiglerus with approval, "but there is nothing like settling these family affairs smoothly."

"Believe me, Wiglerus, I regret the need of his death. I dislike betraying him. I would very much have preferred it if, instead, he had caused your death, at Straithkeld, when he was able to do that."

"In the mouth of Hamlet's wife," Wiglerus assured her, "your sentiments reflect no less credit upon the tender heart than the staunch loyalty of womankind as the highest known sub-division of fauna. And yet—"

He desisted; but the needs of her present position he, as it were, enlightened with the radiancy of his urbane grinning.

"And yet, as an intelligent person," she assented, "I know Hamlet is sunk in fortune beyond any deliverance. I can see that your comfort now demands his death."

Wiglerus inclined to discriminate rather more nicely.

"It is not quite an ignoble stolid question of my mere comfort,—or at least it is not simply that. Where, Hermetrude, is the heroic side of your nature? We have to consider this matter in its more high-minded aspects. All Denmark knows that at Straithkeld your present over-impetuous bedfellow struck me in the face. So public opinion demands that my feelings should remain lacerated, all day and all night, until my vengeance has been glutted. Who am I, to defy public opinion?"

"You are but clay in the hands of the potter," she replied, slowly, from behind the gray blankness of her veil; "and your speaking reminds me, Wiglerus, that my feelings too must be considered."

"You refer, no doubt—my dear niece,—to the modified anguish of becoming a self-made widow?"

"Yes, my uncle; for this bereavement will have its unpleasant side; and so, to extenuate it, you must make me your wife and Queen over Denmark."

He replied with deliberation: "As our good Magnus here has no doubt told you, Hermetrude, I agree to the terms set by your Scots liking for a sound bargain. And I shall hold to these terms strictly. Yet in my capacity as your uncle—"

Hermetrude laughed. She put back her gray veil, displaying that intrepid handsomeness which Wiglerus still regarded with complete æsthetic approval.

"Then our bargain is struck," she declared, "and you, my dear lord, behold your future bride. It is strange that we two should come together at the last—is it not?—after so many sad misunderstandings."

"Pardon me," says Wiglerus; "but at no time have we two misunderstood each other. We have too much in common. Meanwhile, as I was going on to observe, in my capacity as your uncle, it is my duty to give you good advice, even though it should make against my success as your lover. I am not sure that you would further your true interests by marrying me."

She replied, with tender reproof: "You must permit me to be the best judge of my own heart-affairs. I have always liked you, dear rogue, even when you were only a landless vagabond, and when I did not wish to like you. Yet I was swept off my feet, as it were, by the force of a passion too strong for me to resist."

"Yes," said Wiglerus: "it was then that I continued to respect you just as much as ever."

"But now," she went on, "now that you have become King of Denmark, I find both you and my strange liking for you to be still more irresistible."

He inclined his head, with complacent gravity, in acknowledgment of the Queen's kindness.

"And I," says Wiglerus, "need I mention the circumstance that from the first I have adored you? Yet I fear that, even with your liking and my adoration to build upon, our married felicity would be brief. If you should bring me the head of Hamlet, as your dowry, then I would marry you with all fitting honors; and with that nominal appearance of not ever breaking his word which it is the need of a king to display conspicuously, I would keep faith by permitting you to reign as Queen of Denmark, let us say, for some twenty minutes. But afterward, my dear,—and all on account of

the same stupid tyranny which compels me to demand Hamlet's head—why, but immediately afterward, I would be compelled to have you killed, because it is likewise a king's need to keep faith with
the conventions of his realm."

She said only, "I do not understand you."

Wiglerus answered, with an apologetic slight
raising of his shoulders:

"I mean that special convention which we
term the law. I mean that same law of the blood-
feud which drove Hamlet out of Jutland after he
had killed Corambus. When any person is murdered, then, by the laws of my kingdom, it becomes
the decreed duty of the nearest male kinsman of the
dead person to kill the murderer if he or she does
not depart out of the kingdom within five days
during summer or within fourteen days during
winter. Now, despite our deplorably strained relations, I remain Hamlet's nearest adult male kinsman. Although it is my fixed duty in honor to kill
him, yet equally it would be my unpleasant duty
to avenge his being killed by anybody else. Your liking and my adoration may well lament the paradox: still, there it is. I would be bound in honor to
kill the boy's killer, no matter with how charming
an assassin he might happen to be favored."

Of a sudden the King's voice changed. He said
now:

"But in killing you upon any imaginable grounds, or upon no grounds whatever, my dear Hermetrude, I would have back of me not merely the law. I would have back of me a force far greater: for I would have back of me the strong stupid tyranny of public opinion, which regards you as Hamlet's whore, and as the wicked supplanter of his true wife, and as the murderess who destroyed Aalborg; and which would declare my throttling you, here and now, to be plain justice."

Hermetrude meditated, with her red lips a little parted. She said then, at the dictate of her sturdy Scots common-sense:

"You are hardly strong enough to throttle me. Moreover—if I contrive my widowhood—it would be permitted you to avert a blood-feud by accepting a payment of weregild. We could marry then without trouble."

Wiglerus shook his head.

"I am not mercenary. That is one of my few engaging traits. I must cherish my better traits. So I would not accept weregild, should you come to me—as I perceive you have come, Hermetrude,— in the purple mourning robes of a king's widow."

"Why, then," she answered, with an approving carefree smile, "in addition to being unmercenary, you have observant eyes and a vast deal of candor. For the last virtue at least, I may thank you. And

so, King Wiglerus, I shall not attempt to bargain
further. I shall instead withdraw bedazzled by the
bright galaxy of your Majesty's virtues."

"Not yet," says Wiglerus.

Her eyebrows went up languidly.

"Is there any more need for us to be talking,
since we cannot reach terms?"

"Yes, Hermetrude. I must tell you we are both
lost persons. If there be any hell attainable by mankind, we have fairly purchased our admittance to
it."

A thought startled by the uncivil turn of
speech, Queen Hermetrude demanded,—

"How?"

He answered, "I, through some patient thinking; and you, through a too impetuous nature—
which I made bold to criticize at Alcluid, you may
remember,—and upon which I relied patiently."

"I regret"—she moistened her lips—"I regret
that I have not as yet the privilege of understanding you."

"I mean only"—was the quiet explanation of
Wiglerus—"that our good Magnus carries, under
his left arm, a round bundle."

The woman too was quiet. She looked at Wiglerus, for some while, with a handsome stolidity
which the King admired without reserve. Her composure was that of an untroubled cow, he found

time to reflect; it was wholly magnificent. Then Hermetrude spread out her fine strong hands in the placating gesture of one who gives over a lost game.

She said, to Magnus: "Unwrap my tribute! And do you lay at the feet of the King of Denmark, of the king of cheats, of this silken swindler, his well earned tribute."

But to Wiglerus she said: "You have conquered. Here as a free gift, without any cost to you, O very thrifty liar, is the proud head of Hamlet, killed while he slept in my bed. His eyes did not stare like that while the man as yet lived and loved me!"

Wiglerus said only: "Gently does it, my dear. If he had continued to live, I would have been forced to destroy both of you. You have been a bit over-hasty. That was your sole error. You have behaved very sensibly, by and large, in ridding yourself of a fatal encumbrance."

"Yes; but in that way," Hermetrude returned with some discontent, "I have put myself in your power."

Wiglerus was horrified.

"In what situation," he demanded, "could you be more safe? or more sure to be lovingly treated? These suspicions pain me; they twist, so to speak, my heart-strings in the same instant that they dis-

rupt my faith in your common-sense; for they
desecrate all the more intimate memories of our
once tender personal friendship. I can but submit
that such suspicions are unworthy of Hermetrude.
I appeal, in brief, to your more calm consideration
of a Harfaager's talent for gratitude. No, my dear:
you have done me an immense service; and for that
service you shall be repaid, in this world, to the utmost of my ability. In the world to come, we must
both shift as we best may. You are an intelligent
woman who, without uttering any useless com-
plaints, has made the best of a bad matrimonial bargain: I am an honest gentleman who has kept faith
in all respects with his personal honor. I imagine
we shall both burn eternally. Let us hope it may
be permitted us to share the same bale-fire."

She replied sombrely, "I do hope that; for
even in hell, Wiglerus, I would find your hypocrisies
amusing; and besides that, to see you in torment
would please me."

"*Odi et amo*," he answered. "That is my case,
precisely. You see, my dear, we really do have a
great deal in common. Very well, then! Our infernal
tryst is set. Meanwhile, I am under no terrestrial
obligation to dispose of you within the next five
days. So let us both give thanks, to Whoever does
live Upstairs, for the fact that I can allow you to
depart to-morrow, in the estate proper to the

Queen of Pictland, with three—or perhaps we had better say, with five—of my very best ships to attend you, provided only that to-morrow you should see fit to return into your own country."

Her face lightened to see the affair thus happily settled, after a half-hour which had displayed its unpleasant aspects. For all that this dried-up grinning slight man had bargained a bit too thriftily even for a Scotswoman, she now at any rate regarded a future untinged with peril. She was thinking—or so Wiglerus imagined—that with freedom, with wealth, and with a prospering kingdom once more at her disposal, she could manage to get his throat slit at leisure; and because of her gratitude she kissed the compliant King of the Danes, saying,—

"You are good."

"I am good-hearted," Wiglerus admitted, as he put a consoling arm about Hermetrude, with unfeigned affection. "I am not certain that all moralists agree it comes to the same thing."

Thus speaking, the King courteously removed the head of her late husband from out of Hermetrude's way; and he dropped it upon the floor at the far end of the room, just where Wiglerus had first seen the corpse of Horvendile. The head rolled sideways, leaving a watery red smear on the rushes; and rested immediately below that part of the tap-

estry which depicted Gunnar in the snake pit of
Atli.

"Now," Wiglerus added cheerily, "now let us
have supper."

They did have supper; and both ate heartily,
after the passing nervous tension, while they talked
with sincere friendliness; and while Magnus, that
adroit executioner, attended to their needs in the
manner of a butler, quietly and with forethought.

38

OF THE DIRGE WHICH MAGNUS BEGAN

THE STORY SAYS THAT HERMETRUDE WITHDREW
to the apartments which, at the King's orders, had
been made ready for her; and that at this time the
King of Denmark said smilingly:

"But no, Magnus; do you leave there, where
it still oozes not over-tidily, the dear head of my
nephew. I wish to consider at leisure the round purchase price of my comfort and of my recleansed
honor and of my magnanimity."

"Yet it is now needful," said Magnus—and his
dark wistful eyes, as Wiglerus noted in sedate wonder, were overbrimming with tears,—"it is needful I should make a dirge for King Hamlet, whom
the hands of his own wife have put out of living."

Wiglerus leaned back; and with his finger-tips
he drummed thoughtfully upon each arm of his
chair.

"Speaking in confidence, Magnus, and with
that candor which is proper between fellow artists,
was the late entrance of King Hamlet into eternal
life accomplished by a mere tyro in assassination?

or have I the privilege to applaud in it a happy
example of your later manner?"

The skald answered: "Alas, my lord King, but
I was not granted the opportunities which an accident of sex gave to Queen Hermetrude. Mark now
the results! This man was stabbed in his sleep. His
head was then hacked off with some three or four
very bungling sword strokes. One clean neat blow
would have sufficed the true artist; whereas the
stabbing was a redundancy. The stabbing was of-
fensive. The stabbing I consider to have been no
whit short of unethical as the gambit to a beheading."

"In brief," said Wiglerus, "I infer that you,
as a specialist in such matters, do not applaud this
murder."

"It was an abominable performance"—rang
out the indignant response. "It was a crime. Dame
Hermetrude would have done far better to entrust
everything to me, for this killing, in more happy
circumstances, might well have been made my mas-
terwork. I have not ever appraised a client more
promising; it would have been my delight to serve
him; for if only his fortune had been equal with
his inward and native parts"—said Magnus with
enthusiasm—"I know not which one of the old
Hebrews or Greeks or Britons might have been
compared with King Hamlet advantageously."

Then Magnus began to speak in a half-hushed, half-chanting voice, now that, from the staring lopped-off head, he had got the inspiration which death gave always; and the skald said:

"Hard fortune followed Hamlet: yet Hamlet vanquished the rough malice of his time; and through lofty actions he has become worthy of a perpetual famousness. One spot alone made dark the nobility of Hamlet: he was not lord of his own affections; and so he doted upon his wife. Alas, but be a hero never so princely and valiant and wise, yet should he regard over-gravely the ties of wedlock, he must then lessen his final credit. This fault was in the great Hercules; King Arthur, who once reigned with much grace and splendor over all Britain, thus impaired his good name; and Solomon likewise, because of his too fond superfluity and his slavishness, and perhaps because of his optimism also, in trying to satiate some six hundred wives—"

But at this point Magnus was interrupted.

"Your dirge begins its birth-pangs so handsomely," declared Wiglerus, "that it would seem criminal for your muse not to be delivered of her prodigy in somewhat more suitable conditions. Solitude, my good Magnus, is the midwife of enduring art. For that reason, do you have the kindness to attend the advent of a masterpiece—and it may be, of my yet further orders—in the hallway outside."

39

OF ORTON: HOW HE DID NOT GIVE ANY MORE ADVICE

So THE LONG GAMING WAS OVER, WIGLERUS RE-
flected; and he had won. His conscience was agreeably unstained. It was not he who had killed his
nephew. His honor too was unstained, now Hamlet was dead; Alftruda was free to marry; and together they might hope to reign over Denmark, in
exceeding comfort, for many years to come, provided just one more person were put out of living.

For Wiglerus to make safe his honor and his
love and the continuance of his power, it had been
necessary that the head of Hamlet should lie where
it now rested. Here Horvendile had been killed;
here, to-night, the troubles which arose out of his
death found their ending. In the tapestry, Högni
the Brave continued to smile while the heart was
being ripped out of his body; in the tapestry, King
Gunnar, enwreathed with serpents, and with his
hands fettered behind him, continued, quite affably, to charm his reptile neighbors by playing
upon the harp with his toes. You inferred that these

Nibelungs also had put faith in urbanity. They heartened you, through the fine polish of their insouciance, to remember that a difficult and awkward business had been concluded, at long last, with a tact and a skillfulness which—as it was a natural comfort to note, on looking back—had not ever missed their aims, or at least not utterly, since the moment when you cut open poor Geruth's fat arm, here in this same room.

Wiglerus had every reason to be content. There were even some firm grounds for a little self-complacence.

"And yet," said Orton, "this bright room seems comfortless. The staring blond blood-dabbled head is not pleasing to look at, now that you have it safe."

"I was wondering," says Wiglerus—who as yet stayed so deep in meditation as to regard this smiling gray intruder without any special sense of surprise—"what went on inside that head? I know that all the heroic deeds of my deceased nephew were prompted by just one error; so the son of Fengon became very famous and—subject of course to your larger information, Orton,—perhaps he became damned also, merely because he believed himself to have been begotten by Horvendile. He died happily, somewhat as did Siward Swift-Foot, under this misapprehension as to his sublime origin."

"Many of my best friends," returned Orton, "are Christians; and their faith seems to content them."

He coughed. Then the gray man continued,—

"Yet the death of Siward Swift-Foot in his high-minded delusion did rather more than to afford a neat parallel for the proud death of Hamlet; for it balanced, quite exactly, my dear Wiglerus, against a son who had killed his own father, a father who had killed his son."

"Let us speak of more pleasant matters," said Wiglerus.

"Ah! but you are biassed," Orton observed regretfully. "Now I, as an amateur of art, I elect to applaud the Norns for their rude and authentic genius in contriving this neat balance. It bespeaks a certain broad-mindedness, I would submit to you, thus to prevent the pot from criticizing the complexion of the kettle. It makes for calmness, in all quarters. But for Siward Swift-Foot my lord King, you would have been falling into Heaven alone might say what strident orgies of harsh moral reproof. As the matter stands, you have, instead, quite quietly, murdered Hamlet also; and these continued small triumphs in the way of homicide your Majesty cannot conceivably but regard as gratifying."

"None the less," Wiglerus answered, "I have

not ever comprehended this big brutal man-child who reached out, no less bravely than greedily, for whatever he desired, without using any tact. Now I must always stay uncertain as to the nature of Hamlet. I know only that Hamlet must be recalled shruggingly, so long as anybody remembers him, as a mere synonym for unreflectiveness and too hasty action."

"You forget," remarked Orton, smiling, "the sustained cunning with which he feigned madness and so got the better of King Fengon."

"One does not need"—Wiglerus generalized—"any unusual cunning to run about making the sound of a condensed menagerie; and at best, this blond tall brute could hardly prove he was not an idiot by behaving like one."

"It was an excellent device," says Orton, with a touch of hurt pride. "Moreover, you forget his most notable magic-working in Britain, by which he revealed matters that were not known to any living man."

Wiglerus said drily, "Perhaps in that soothsaying, which provoked trouble for everybody, a fiend aided him."

"Indeed—or so, at least, I have heard," replied Orton,—"it is not unusual for those philanthropic spirits whom an ungrateful race of mankind calls fiends, to be advising each perplexed human being as to his private interests in this world, and about the likeliest way of securing them. No angel, you must let me remark, is thus generous in pointing out the more profitable misdemeanor. And perhaps the angels have some right on their side: for to give wise advice is dangerous. I know that I gave freely to Hamlet, and to Edric also, the most intelligent sort of advice; and Fengon too I prompted, in some degree, with advice of a plainly rational nature. How lively was my chagrin to observe that the following out of my advice destroyed the three of them, I can but leave to your imagination. I rejoice, Wiglerus, you do not need any advice."

"I prefer to be guided by the obligations of honor," replied Wiglerus frankly,—"with the assistance now and then of my common-sense."

"So that, at the last, your most gracious Majesty has deceived Queen Hermetrude, very mercifully, for her comfort's sake?"

"It may be that I do not understand you, Orton," the King said in undisguised wonder. "I told her—and as I thought, I told her quite plainly —that both my honor and the laws of my kingdom left me the power, for five days as yet, to permit her to return into Pictland unmolested."

"Yet you did not tell her, it should be observed,

that you meant to exercise this power. A Nordic gentleman does not ever tell any downright lies, except in secrecy to his own conscience," declared Orton approvingly.

"I left open the door of equivocation," Wiglerus agreed, "in case I had need of it. For the hard fact remains that if I permit Hermetrude to go out of my kingdom alive, the death of Hamlet will stay unavenged by me, who am his nearest of adult male kin; and that it may be said I connived at, or even prompted, his killing."

"Now, but indeed, my lord King,"—and Orton, shook his gray head commiseratingly,—"in a world so censorious and so very quick to speak malice about eminent persons, some ugly scandal of that sort is not improbable."

"And in that case, Orton, then by-and-by, when young Eric reaches manhood, there must be a blood-feud between me and the son of Hamlet, who happens likewise to be the child of Alftruda. Inasmuch as I intend to marry Alftruda, that would be inconvenient."

Orton smiled now, benignantly, and with a warm-heartedness begotten by an assured faith in human nature.

"With the child in your daily keeping, Wiglerus, and with the fate of poor King Fengon in your recollection, your stepson would not reach manhood."

Wiglerus answered: "The seductive and accomplished spirits of evil think of everything in advance. So, within the confines of my more modest abilities, do I. And I have found in my mind a new and not wholesome tendency to hover about poisons. Should I grant myself the pleasure of keeping entire faith with poor Hermetrude's expectations, then in mere common-sense I must contrive the death of little Eric—as painlessly as may be, of course, and without arousing Alftruda's suspicions. I could manage it without any special trouble. It is upon the whole the most simple solution, and the rational settlement. Yet it has, I admit, an unpleasant side. I regret my need to kill the boy. You see, Orton, I have grown rather fond of young Eric."

"I may safely urge you, in the light of that urbane fondness," returned Orton, "to become heroic. Do you abstain from yet further assassination; let Eric live; entrust all to the wisdom of Heaven; and accept bravely the result of your own doings."

"And thus bring about my own destruction! or at any rate, my own personal discomfort!" says Wiglerus, in his shocked surprise. "Ah, no, my poor unperceptive devil! your arts fail you; for in middle-age no intelligent human person stays heroic. He can but hope, at best, to retain some little aversion to his own daily doings."

"Your apothegm," Orton replied pensively, "recalls to me yet another saying, which I overheard no great while ago. 'When that happens, the man is dead; and though his body may go on breathing, it is but the body of an animal—oh, a quite harmless and good-tempered animal perhaps— which continues to eat and to breed and to sleep, not discontentedly.' "

Thus speaking, Orton took up his cane of orange-wood.

"At all events," says he, with a friendly smile of admiring congratulation, "that fairly satisfied and fairly successful destroyer of youth does not any longer need my advice in this world. And for the rest, King Wiglerus, my interest in the affairs of your family has been philosophic. Some while ago you paused to confer a few idle compliments upon Earl Sigmund's wife, because she had a pleasingly tinted hide. It has entertained me to follow out the results. And that—that, for the present— is all. To our next meeting, King Wiglerus!"

Thus amicably, and with so little ostentation as to make his leaving become hardly noticeable, the benevolent gray cripple went away from this bright room, where at the King's feet lay the head of the King's enemy, and a prospering and honor-laden future awaited the high King of Denmark, if only, by contriving to put the son of Hamlet also out of living, he continued to act tactfully.

40

ENDING OF THE STORY OF HAMLET: WITH THE VERDICT OF KING WIGLERUS, THE SON OF RÖREK

We tell about how Wiglerus came to the home of Alftruda, at Thorë, after his day's work had been finished. She walked slowly across the small green lawn to meet the discreetly debonair King of Denmark. In the golden light of sunset he observed her loveliness, or at any rate her entire lovableness, and the grave affection with which she regarded him. At her side—half clinging to plump Alftruda, but smiling shyly upward, toward his funny uncle —came young Eric; about whom Wiglerus had no further reason to bother, now that the King's mind had become reconciled to the child's doom. The boy's nurse attended them.

Wiglerus, by and large, was content. With the one last need of a most awkward position disposed of, he might hope (as his thinking phrased it, with a neatly poetic touch) to enjoy a fair season of domestic happiness in the golden sunset of his living. Nothing whatever perturbed Wiglerus, except that he did find something oddly familiar in the face of Eric's nurse. He asked her name.

The woman answered him, "I am called Thora, Majesty; and when my husband lived, I was the wife of Earl Sigmund of Lökken."

"I remember you," says Wiglerus; and he looked pensively at the source of his former innocent pleasures.

She had not any trace of her first youth remaining, he observed. A blurred large scar disfigured her right cheek, where it had been burned at the siege of Aalborg. Two of her upper teeth were missing; and that which she had endured while being raped at Aalborg, by seven or eight hurried soldiers, had made gray her hair and had left dull the eyes of Thora Fairskin. The marvellous skin was dingy looking now, and everywhere it was blotched with brown spottings.

It seemed to Wiglerus a sad happening that the pure soft colors, the frail prettiness of youth, which had altered so many lives familiar to him, should have passed out of this world as utterly as had Horvendile and Corambus and Fengon and Edric and Hamlet, along with so many other persons, all whom, without her ever knowing about it, this woman's lost prettiness had led to be destroyed. It was perhaps a mere accident too—reflected Wiglerus,—that he had not loved this woman instead of Alftruda. But for the death of Horvendile, he would have remained at young Thora's elbow, deep in philandering; and he would have fallen, more or less gravely, and perhaps forever, in love with this woman, this disfigured, ageing and wholly commonplace woman.

Human life seemed astoundingly casual; you could not find any meaning in it; but you could find in human life a quite ponderable amount of pleasure, through the exercise of continued tact. That, and that only, might enable you, for some while as yet to come, to eat and to breed and to sleep not at all discontentedly (just as Orton had said), in a world full of human beings who were far less intelligent and more unhappy than you were,—such luckless creatures as this Thora Fairskin, for example.

"I remember you well, dear lady," said Wiglerus; and a thought surprisingly, the high King of Denmark bent downward, with a tinge of sorrow, to kiss the toil-roughened hand of a rather ugly drynurse.

After that, he touched the boy's flaxen head, very lightly, with a gesture which the King knew to be sacrificial. He noted thus how like, in its long oval shaping, was the child's head to the head of Hamlet; and put aside the unpleasant thought.

Yet Wiglerus noted also the confiding alert

smile which Eric had flashed upward. This small
fair imp was without distrust of any living creature, and no lasting griefs troubled young Eric. It
seemed to Wiglerus an inexpedient happening that
youth and the bright cleanness of youth should go
slowly out of this child; or that time's handling
should ever tarnish and deface and degrade the
child's fine purity, very much as time had made
dingy the transient prettiness of poor Thora Fairskin, and as time had made dim a very far-away
young Wiglerus, and as time made less wonderful
all youthfulness, both of body and mind. Yes: before that had happened, it would, in reality, be far
more kind to Eric, the King assured himself, to put
an end to young Eric.

Wiglerus shrugged. You could not afford to
be kindly, in this special case. You could not, with
any real comfort, leave open even the bare possibility of Alftruda's ever finding out about your
kindness in killing her child. Alftruda would be
quite unreasonable about your kindness. So had it
become the sad need of Wiglerus to be implacable;
and to permit Eric to go on living until chance
and time had disposed of, and had turned dingy,
all his fineness; and had made of him, in brief, just
another well-meaning sordid Wiglerus; and by-and-
by had made out of this Eric (as out of this Wiglerus) nothing.

With that settled, the King smiled at Alftruda, whom he no longer loved with any passionate ador-, ing, and knew to be as commonplace as was Thora Fairskin, but whom he did not desire to have changed in any particular; and the heart of Wiglerus glowed, temperately but agreeably.

"Hamlet is dead, my dearest," the King remarked; "he is as dead as young Wiglerus. I do not know of any more exact synonym for extinction."

He sighed; and then added, with a gesture of reassurance:

"But I have avenged my nephew honorably. And his murderess did not suffer at all—as it is a melancholy pleasure to reflect,—because in such matters our good Magnus is skillful. He murdered Hermetrude in her sleep last night, under my supervision, without any least disturbance. It follows that every moral obligation is satisfied; and that you and I can be married to-morrow. In brief—as I promised you at Middleburgh, Alftruda,—the saga of Wiglerus is ending upon an edifying note, after all, and quite happily. It ends indeed like an old fairy tale"—said the urbane King of Denmark, as he put a consoling arm about his Alftruda, very much as last night he had embraced Hermetrude,— "with virtue attaining to its just reward, and with true love winning its desired recompense."

EXPLICIT

"Here is our colophon, for here endeth the story of Hamlet and his uncle. The narrator of it beseeches you that shall read this history not to resemble the spider who feedeth of the corruption that she findeth in the spoiled leaves and fruits which are in the garden, where the bee gathereth her honey out of the best and fairest flowers she can light upon. A man that is well brought up should read the lives of these whoremongers, drunkards, incestuous, violent and bloody persons, not to follow their missteps, and so to defile himself with wickedness, but to take pattern by the unwisdom of Hamlet in this discourse; who erred in that he loved over-greatly; and who, while others made lax cheer, continued sober and ardent; so that, where the more nimble wits of his fellows sought as much as they could to get pleasure and treasure, he accounted not anything to be equal to honor."